...And She Laughed

Volume I

*She is Powerful, Fearless,
Victorious...She is YOU!!*

Anesha A. Sharp

...And She Laughed ~ Volume I
Copyright © 2015 Anesha A. Sharp

Cover Design by SW Designs Studio
Edited by Joy M. Thomas, Ph.D

Library of Congress Catalog-in-Publication Data

Sharp, Anesha A.

…And She Laughed / Anesha A. Sharp
   p. cm.

ISBN: 0692458395
ISBN-13: 978-0692458396

Printed in the United States of America

Contents

Contents

Dedication

In my lifetime, I have had the privilege of having a front row seat observing the experiences of many dynamic, beautiful and amazing women. I've seen their struggles, heard their cries and felt their pain, but on an equal scale, I've seen them overcome, be triumphant and continue to live even when they thought they might die. The strength that is in a woman leaves me in utter awe I don't even think we understand the care God used to create us and the power he equipped us with. Think about this for a second: it was a woman that God the creator of the universe entrusted His most precious seed, Jesus! Let that sit with you for a minute.

As you read these women's narratives of strength, courage, and the ability to reach for that which is within them, see the same in yourself. Maybe your journey isn't the exact experiences of the women in this book, but in some way I believe you will be able to connect with them. This book is dedicated to the celebration of your life my dear sister! Yes, you reading these words—I celebrate YOU!

Acknowledgments

Father God, thank you for birthing this book in my spirit a number of years ago and for keeping the fire blazing inside me until its delivery. I'm ever grateful and humbled that you would choose to use me for such an impactful purpose! I pray I make you proud!

Tavatchai Sharp, what a man, husband and father you are! I thank you for always making space for my dreams! Thank you for your love and support over the years that has allowed me to freely birth the purpose God has put inside me. I love you!

Pastor, Boss, Spiritual Father and Mentor Charles Martin, I thank God for you! It has been your ministry that has increased my faith to believe for what God put inside me to produce with me life! Thank you for personally walking me through so many aspects of my life that has prepared me for destiny!

Dr. Joy Thomas, thank you for your help on this project! You are anointed and amazing at what you do!

Brittany Clay, I owe you a huge thank you! In seasons when I didn't feel like writing your funny reminders encouraged me! I greatly appreciate you!

To the people who have been my sounding board in any way on this project, there's so many to name, but you know who you are: THANK YOU!

PART ONE

Faith

Introduction: Faith

If you're honest with yourself you can admit with me that you've had a moment in time that challenged your faith or core beliefs. An experience so ghastly that it may have caused your knees to buckle and breathe to wane. A time that left you questioning and sometimes screaming, *"God why me?! Do you really see me?! Do you even care!?"* I've been there, frightened and feeling alone, grasping in the dark hoping someone will see me, find me...HELP ME!

In the story of Faith we find Vanessa in that obscure place. She's given up on her faith due to a very tragic event in her life, but she doesn't realize the chain of events that are about to capture her life will change her forever!

Chapter

1

THE DREAM

She lay awake wrestling between reality and the dream world; drenched from cold sweats, she arose quickly from her sleep. With a sudden ease, she went to the restroom. The dream had been disturbing. She had the same dream three nights in a row and tonight she realized maybe God, the universe, or something was trying to speak to her. Quietly, creeping to the kitchen as not to wake anyone up, she decided to grab a snack and ponder this reoccurring dream. *What had this all meant*? She wondered. As she reached for the last piece of chocolate cake she made earlier, she jumped as she felt warmth on her neck. Vanessa turned around and to her surprise stood her tall and handsome husband.

Michael still gave her chills, even after 12 years of marriage. At times, it was as though they were still in the honeymoon phase of their marriage. Theirs was a match made in...well, she would say heaven, but she wasn't sure if she believed in such a place. She used to until her mother passed away seven years ago, now she struggled with what she believed. Vanessa knew there was something out there, but that something had let her down one too many times, and her mother's passing was the last straw.

Michael was the best thing that had happened in her life. Early on, they decided not to have children because it would only complicate their already busy and ambitious lives. He was a successful attorney with his own law practice that he owned with his older and younger brothers. The team was known for winning high profile and celebrity cases. She was a successful interior designer with a business that specialized in designing for big businesses and the wealthy. Life for them was hectic and fast paced. However, they did find the time to care for their two miniature yorkie-poos, well not really, their housekeeper did that; but they did get to enjoy their fun and exciting personalities when they were home.

As she turned around to catch her husband standing behind her, he kissed her lips gently, "Honey why are you out of bed? Is everything okay?" She looked long and deep into his green eyes, she wanted to be honest, she longed to tell him the truth. Vanessa never kept anything from her husband, but she knew now wasn't the right time. "Honey," he said, "What's the matter? You're scaring me with that strange look on your face."

"Oh," now aware of the blank expression she held, with the truth and the lie both on her tongue, in one breath she reached for the lie, "Everything is okay. I just had a hard time getting back to sleep once I went to the restroom, and you know how much I love my chocolate cake." She thought about her mom as she took the next bite, it had been her recipe. Although Vanessa rarely cooked, when she found the time, she made things that reminded her of her mother. Michael reached over and lovingly wiped the chocolate icing from the corner of her mouth, licked his finger, and smiled. She laughed; he always knew how to make her laugh.

"Well, baby I'm going back to bed, join me soon. I'm missing you next to me," with that he glanced at her once more to make sure all was well with her. Somehow he knew everything wasn't okay, but he was a patient man and he knew in time all would be revealed; she couldn't keep anything from him for too long. He leaned over gathered her soft face in his hands, kissed the bridge of her nose, and then her forehead twice and proceeded to the bedroom.

Vanessa was 5 foot 2 and beyond gorgeous. She could have been a model, but she always felt she was too short. She was the type of woman that when she walked in a room everyone noticed including the women, but she never tried to demand too much attention, although she did enjoy it. She was naturally who she was and she made no apologies for it. She wore her curly hair just past her shoulders. She used to wear it straight when she wore a relaxer, but she hadn't done that in almost seven years, and she was pleased with the change. It was so much easier on her constantly demanding lifestyle. Vanessa worked out regularly and her easy going hairstyle gave her more versatility.

Vanessa was a caramel color with skin that always seemed to glow. She wore a tad bit of makeup, but it was never needed and although she had just turned 43 last month, she didn't look a day older than 27. Sometimes she still got carded when she wanted to enjoy a glass of wine at her favorite restaurants. On her tiny frame she carried 102 pounds. Last year she gave up on her dream of weighing 115 pounds, she couldn't even make it to 105 pounds. To many her size would've been a gift, but not for her, she hated being so small. Vanessa often pictured herself much bigger; she wasn't sure why, maybe it boosted her ego a bit.

She slowly ate her cake and drank her milk; she wanted to buy herself a little more time before heading to bed. During mid-bite, in strolls Diamond, her dog, she knew Bentley, Michael's dog would soon be following. He went everywhere Diamond went. Vanessa knew Bentley would rather stay in their little beds asleep, but she knew he couldn't resist knowing what Diamond would be up to. She scooped Diamond up in her lap and caressed her fur. Diamond being the greedy love sponge that she was, yawned, looked down at Bentley and lazily stretched her tiny body out over Vanessa's entire lap, as to send a silent message that she wasn't going to share her comfy spot. The message was received, Bentley curled up on the floor next to Vanessa's fluffy soft pink slippers.

Vanessa finished her cake, rose with Diamond in hand, cleaned the island area where she ate her cake, and proceeded to take Diamond to her bed with Bentley following on her heels. She laid Diamond down and Bentley curled up in his bed next to Diamond. Vanessa reached over to caress Bentley's fur before rising to walk away.

She walked into their dark bedroom, gradually feeling her way to the bed, her eyes hadn't adjusted to the intense light change. She glanced at the clock and sighed, it read 3:55 AM; she had to be up in a few more hours. She silently slipped into bed. Somehow, Michael, who had been asleep almost an hour, sensed her presence, rolled over to scoop her up and pull her close into him. She looked at Michael who was still asleep and she wondered how he did that. It never failed. If he went to bed before her he always knew—even in his sleep when she came to bed. But, even after 12 years of marriage it didn't annoy her, she felt safe and she loved that feeling.

Hearing the all too familiar sound of the alarm clock jolted Vanessa out of her sleep, *if two hours of sleep could be called that*, she thought. After her nap of a sleep she wanted so badly to hit the snooze button, but she knew she needed her full hour and a half to get ready so she promptly got up! Her husband always woke up an hour before her; he liked having what he called his "quite time with God". During this time he read his bible and prayed; he prayed for his day, concerns he had, and for his wife. Quiet as it's kept, sometimes he even went into where she was sleeping, gently laid his hand on her chest and prayed for her. He always ended his quiet time giving thanks to God for the beautiful life he was allowed to live!

He had been a person of prayer ever since she had known him. Michael had grown up in a Baptist church and the principles of prayer that had been passed down from generations had followed him throughout the years. He had often been quoted telling friends and colleagues that his very eventful life as an attorney kept him on his knees.

Michael's desire to continue in his faith had amazed Vanessa because he, like her, had experienced many bumpy roads, but somehow he still managed to believe. What she loved about him is he didn't force her to be like him. He always gave her space to find her way, but what she didn't know is that he knew that she would always find her way back to where she needed to be. Michael never feared for one moment when she had decided to, as she put it "divorce God."

Michael was always so considerate of her; he kept warm coffee along with the morning paper, which he had already thumbed through, on the kitchen counter awaiting her arrival. Entering the kitchen all dressed and smelling of her favorite perfume that left a pleasant scent even after she exited a room, she grabbed her coffee and slowly sipped it while sliding her feet into her size 36 (size 6 US) Louboutin heels.

In walked the sexiest man she'd ever seen. She often wondered how she had gotten so lucky and even though she wasn't a bad catch herself, she could have never imagined marrying such a beautiful specimen of a man. Towering over her petite frame at 6 foot 3 inches tall, he made Boris Kodjoe look like an afterthought with all his handsomeness. In his younger days he was an underwear print ad model and he never lost his alluring looks. Michael's butter scotch tinted skin and piercing green eyes almost gave her heart palpitations the first time they locked eyes many years ago. He had recently joined the ranks of distinguished gentlemen—growing a little bit of salt in his pepper colored hair, but it didn't distract from his looks one bit. Still sporting a very chiseled body and abs, to say he was fine was an understatement!

He walked over to her licked his lips and said, "Baby, spin for me, I wanna full view!" He was always such a flirt and she loved it! She slowly rose to her feet attempting to channel her inner sexy for a moment and gave her husband a slow sexy modelesque turn.

"Ooh baby!" He said as he smiled.

She couldn't keep it up much longer, he still made her feel shy at times. "Honey!" She said with a bashful smile.

"Okay baby, I'm done lusting after you for now. I'd better get to work before we start some extracurricular activities that will make both of us late!" He said with a chuckle. They walked over to the door leading to the garage and kissed, he turned on the house alarm and off to work they went.

Chapter

2

"WHY CAN'T I SHAKE IT?"

Secured in her sleek black Mercedes E-Class Sedan, she began to revisit the dream again. *Why can't I shake it and why does it keep reoccurring?* She wondered. *There must be someone I can talk to, I need to get it off my mind.* Just then, she pushed a button on her car phone, it rang four times before a familiar voice on the other end said, "Hello!"

Denise was her longest-standing friendship. It had endured through many great times and many tough moments. She could always count on Denise and Denise knew the same of Vanessa.

"Hey girl, what are your plans for lunch today?"

Denise glanced at her calendar, "Actually, I'm free!" She said with excitement. Denise was always upbeat and happy, no matter what she faced, she knew how to command life and that was one thing Vanessa always loved about her, an attribute she wished she had.

"Great, meet me for lunch at Isabella Seven!" Vanessa was always one to get straight to the point; she didn't have a lot of time for small talk. As she ended the phone call, her sun glasses fell from her hand and in her haste to retrieve them, she took her eyes off the road. She shifted her eyes back to the road as she heard a loud horn and to her horror, she had veered into oncoming traffic and was now about to be plowed head on by a large red SUV. She yelled out, "Oh God!" and swerved just in enough time not to be the next car wreck on the 5 o'clock news. Vanessa was shocked that her car hadn't hit the large suburban that was headed directly for her. She knew it had to have been an act of God or had it? Why would He choose to appear now after all the other things that she needed Him to do? *How dare He conveniently show up now?* She thought.

Vanessa kept watching the clock and waiting for lunch, she could hardly focus on any of her work and she needed to talk to her favorite friend immediately. She had some new contracts to write, but how could she focus with today's events and that crazy dream? Not being one to procrastinate, she promised herself she would do it after lunch or maybe she would have her assistant Cindy work on it while she was out. Cindy had been with her for as long as she had been in business and she trusted her, but the perfectionist in her wouldn't allow Cindy to touch certain very important and very lucrative contracts. Cindy knew her boss's idiosyncrasies, but she understood Vanessa so it didn't bother her one bit. In fact, Cindy simply gave her and all her quirkiness space to exist without any pressure. She loved Vanessa and had the utmost respect for her, in return Vanessa was a great boss to her. What really put Vanessa at ease is Cindy knew how to handle her staff when she was away.

The clock struck 11:17am. *That's it, this morning is creeping along. I will just head over early*, Vanessa thought. She knew Denise would be late by at least 10 minutes, it was her custom, but this time Vanessa didn't care. She had to get out of her office, what she really wanted was to get out of her head, unfortunately that wasn't a possibility. Her head was where she lived most of the time. Her mom used to tell her not to take life so seriously, learn to laugh more and enjoy the simple things, but for some reason it was very difficult for her to do. Her mother was a free spirit like Denise; she often wondered if that was the reason she kept her around for so long. One thing Vanessa was known for was getting rid of people. If they caused her too much pain or made her life too difficult, they were on the next spaceship to the moon. Her marriage to Michael for so many years was a pure miracle.

Grabbing her favorite Prada purse, she picked up her phone and buzzed Cindy, "Hey, I'm heading out to an early meeting with a client." *Dang it*, she thought, *why did I lie and why did it roll of my tongue so easily?* "I will be back soon," she continued. *Darn it another lie, what's the deal with me today?* She wondered. "I'm going to Isabella Seven, would you like anything back or can I grab you some sushi on my way in?" Vanessa asked.

"Ummm," Cindy responded. She wondered why Vanessa lied, then again she thought why wonder? Vanessa was a private person when it came to her personal life and she went to great measures to keep even the simplest things a secret. Even when Vanessa purchased new clothes, she never wanted to be labeled "the pretty girl who was addicted to shopping" even though that was mostly true, she hardly ever said anything was new when asked. In addition to understanding Vanessa, she respected her privacy and never tried to unravel her web of secrets and little white lies. "Sure, I'll take some sushi, the special," she said.

"Okay girl. See you soon," Vanessa responded. Cindy knew that meant working through lunch, but she always left her schedule open for those days and Vanessa always made sure she ate well on her tab. On the brighter side Cindy knew that she would get to leave 30 minutes to an hour early the next day.

On the road again Vanessa was dodging through traffic, she knew she was anxious, but she couldn't figure out why. Not to mention that Denise wasn't going to be anywhere near on time, nevertheless she zoomed past cars as she sped all the way to the restaurant. Then it dawned on her while she was approaching the restaurant that earlier that morning she had almost been scraped off the side of the road. "Well if You did save me, thanks!" She said aloud in a rude voice. Pulling up to the sign that read, 'Valet Parking' she said, "Wait what am I doing? Why am I talking to myself? There's no one up there and if there was He surely doesn't care about me." Forgetting about the gentlemen outside her vehicle waiting to park it, she sighed and adjusted her review mirror and fixed her lip gloss. She wanted to take the care needed to make sure she didn't look like she felt.

"Okay, I'm going to go in here, clear my head and I will be totally fine after I talk to Denise. She will help me sort all this out." *At least I hope so,* she thought. She looked over at the time in her car; it read 11:44 AM. She was surprised that she made it so fast. She was known as a cautious and slow driver, all her friends including her husband teased her and called her "the turtle". But, not today she turned what normally took her 35 minutes into a 24 minute drive. *Surely I wasn't driving that fast,* she thought *or maybe I normally drive really slow,* she chuckled at herself. She slowly slid out of her car, giving the gentlemen with the sour look on his face her keys. She wondered what was wrong with him, lost in her own world she hadn't realized that he had been standing outside her car waiting on her for close to ten minutes.

Chapter

3

THE REVEAL

Seated in the restaurant she adjusted her clothes, smoothing her skirt yet one more time and fixing her blouse after the fifteenth time. In walks Denise 10 minutes late just as she had predicted. She stood and motioned for Denise, although she wasn't sure she could put it all into words, Vanessa was sure that after her wait she would be ready to tell it all. The one thing she struggled with was being in touch with how she felt and talking about it was even worse. They hugged and Denise took a seat.

After an hour of picking at her eggplant parmigiana, Vanessa intently held on to every word Denise said. Denise was such a great story teller, Vanessa attributed it to the fact that she was a world renowned inspirational speaker and she simply never ran out of words. Vanessa was sure she talked in her sleep and to every item or being she came into contact with. Denise loved to talk, it was one of the things that complemented their friendship so well because

Vanessa loved to listen and she was great at it. Letting her mind take a small intermission while Denise talked about her latest excursion to Alaska, Vanessa contemplated whether she could actually share the dream with her friend.

"Girl, I knew this time was the right time for me to do it. I've been to Alaska several times and each time I said I would ski only to get there and coward out, but this time John wasn't having it, he made sure I did it!"

Vanessa was happy for Denise! Since she had known Denise that was the first time she had ever seen her love a man enough to let her guard down a bit. She was just waiting for the moment when Denise would announce their engagement. Just when Vanessa thought Denise had forgotten the reason for their meeting, she blurts out, "So um, what's the urgency lady, are you pregnant?"

Vanessa choked on the water she was sipping on. "Wh, wh what, why would you say that?! Of course I'm NOT pregnant, you know what Michael and I decided on years ago! I just can't believe you'd say that," Vanessa said angrily.

"Whoa, I was only joking, take a breather," Denise said with a warm smile, trying to calm her down. She always knew how to handle her best friend when she went over the edge.

Vanessa breathed in deep, composing herself, "Girl I'm sorry, I've just had a crazy morning." Vanessa said in an attempt to smooth things over and not look like she was trying to hide anything.

Denise reached over and put her hand on top of Vanessa, "So honey what's going on? Over the phone you sounded like there was something you really needed to talk about." Vanessa's eyes were fixed on Denise's, but she wasn't really looking at her at all, she was in a daze, thinking of the dream and the morning's events. She wasn't quite ready to divulge the dream, so instead she told Vanessa about the close call car accident that shook her up that morning, minus the part about the conversation with God. As obviously traumatic as the event had sounded, Denise couldn't help but wonder if there was more, something that had really shaken Vanessa to her soul. Not wanting to belittle what had taken place that morning, Denise avoided asking her, "is that all?" which is what she really wanted to say. They chatted a little while longer then Denise and Vanessa hugged once again before departing ways and scheduling a couple's dinner next week at Denise's new house.

Back at the office after an almost three hour lunch break, she gave Cindy her sushi and retreated to her office. Vanessa hit it hard for the next two hours. She enlisted Cindy's help to knock out two new contracts she had received the week prior, one was for a multi - million dollar home and the other was for a new women's boutique. After they completed the contacts they were both exhausted mentally. Cindy locked up and they headed home. On her drive home Vanessa decided she was going to talk to Michael about her dream. She was relieved that he would be getting off of work late which would give her enough time to gather her thoughts and be prepared to tell him all about it.

Relaxed in a warm bubble bath, she gazed in a blur at the tea light candles on her wall and she watched as each little flame danced and flickered to its own tune. She slowly closed her eyes thinking of the dream, she smiled lovingly and touched her stomach. *Hmmm, it was a nice thought*, she said within herself. Vanessa opened her eyes and was pleased to be back in reality. She sipped her wine that had been waiting on her at the edge of the bath tub. The soft sound of Luther Vandross playing in the background soothed her, she enjoyed his voice. His music always relaxed her after a long day's work. With ease she placed her wine glass back to its resting place and picked up her book entitled, *'In The Shadows'*. It was a mystery book. She loved putting herself in the place of the detective, secretly she used to want to be one.

She closed her book just in time to hear the timer on the oven alerting her that her turkey loaf, her husband's favorite, was ready. She had forgotten that she had put it in the oven right before she got ready to get in the tub. She bolted to the kitchen in her white fluffy robe and hair wrapped in a towel. The moment she hit the kitchen she was smacked in the face by the aroma of the turkey loaf, the smell immediately made her hungry! She grabbed her oven mittens and pulled her dinner from the oven, trailing behind her heels was Diamond and Bentley.

She finished everything for the late meal and put on some sexy lingerie. She found her husband's favorite red lingerie and slipped it on. Although they had made love regularly at least 2 to 3 times a week, she wasn't trying to advertise for sex or to get him aroused. Tonight she wanted to have a long stimulating conversation and her husband loved to see her in sexy lingerie, it always relaxed him instantly after work.

Lying across her bed in her sexy best with her leopard slippers she looked up at the ceiling day dreaming, when she heard the garage go up. She promptly sprang from her trance and ran to the restroom; she wanted to make sure she still looked the way she remembered 25 minutes ago. As she hoped, every hair was in place and her bare face with just a hint of lip gloss still looked flawless. She pulled out her favorite diamond earrings he had bought her a few years ago for their wedding anniversary and sprayed her perfume in front of her and walked through its mist. This late at night she wanted to have a hint of his favorite perfume on, but not too strong, just enough to tantalize his nose. Taking a little longer than she had intended, when she stepped out the restroom, in walked her life saver.

"Oh," she said startled to see him, he stood in the doorway admiring his eye candy.

"Girl, you know the type of medicine I'm in need of tonight," He said jokingly—yet serious!

"Oh baby," she said stepping up on her tippy toes to kiss his neck, she didn't want him to notice the strange expression on her face. He knew by the way she kissed him that today wasn't a sex night, but a 'let's talk night'. He didn't mind because after all if he listened very well and was really attentive, which would be easy to do with her looking so sexy, he would definitely be going to sleep satisfied.

"Ok, baby let me get changed and I will be in to talk with you. I'm interested to hear what's going on in that beautiful mind," he said with a soft smile. She loved that he knew her so well.

"Ok honey, I'm going to go light the candles on the dining room table. I made turkey loaf!" She said with excitement as she exited. *Oh*, he thought, she had him in such a trance he didn't even notice the smell of dinner. Now taking note of the pleasing fragrance he was even more aroused. A sexy dinner? What more could a man ask for? Oh yeah sex, with that thought, he laughed out loud.

Walking into the formal dining room with a smile, he sat down to his plate already made and looking very delicious while eyeing the love of his life who looked even more delicious. "Baby, you cooked for the second night this week and it's only Tuesday, to what do I owe this?" Michael asked surprised.

"I don't know, I guess I've just been in a cooking mood lately," she responded. She couldn't hold it in another second, she blurted out, "What do you think of kids?"

"Um, let's see. I think they're cute, funny, and noisy as fire crackers on the Fourth of July. Oh and very messy, have you ever changed a diaper with runny poop, oooh weee?" He stopped mid-bite to look at his very serious and silent wife who hadn't even cracked a smile at one of his sarcastic jokes.

"I, I, I mean what do you think of having kids?" She asked. At that the food flew out of his mouth, he was in no way prepared for such a question.

"Baby," he said slowly grabbing her hand, "Umm are you preg...pregnant?" He managed to force out of his mouth.

"Well, no. I mean I don't think so," She replied.

"You don't think so?! Well honey, what's with the question, did I miss something? I thought we, I mean *you* didn't want kids?" He asked, cleaning up the food he had just spit out and trying to gather his thoughts. This wasn't exactly how he had expected the night to go.

"No, you're right, I just wondered what you thought, if your mind had somehow, you know, changed. No big deal, I definitely don't want any children that's for sure," she said as she began to lift the fork to her lips. He wanted to say more, ask more questions, he desperately wanted to know what was going on in her head. He needed to understand her change of heart, but he was afraid to know the answer so he continued stuffing his mouth with food. Somehow, he sensed the conversation was far from over. After dinner she cleaned the kitchen. Vanessa decided she did want that tall, handsome husband of hers to make love to her. After today's occurrences she needed the soothing touch that only he could give.

She walked into the bedroom where he was getting undressed. Vanessa came up behind Michael and kissed him lightly on his exposed back. Michael grinned, slowly turned around to face his bride and then swept her up in his arms. Carrying her over to the bed, without any words he laid her across it. He was relieved he hadn't pursued anymore of the disturbing conversation. Now the concern the conversation left him with and the cares of the day would be washed away in her love. With his piece of heaven on earth secured tightly in his arms, he felt at peace sharing the art of love with his soul mate as he pressed his lips tenderly against hers.

Sleeping peacefully in her husband's arms, Vanessa awakened suddenly in another cold sweat and ran to the kitchen. *What is happening to me?* She thought as she shook her head. "Leave me the hell alone!" she yelled as she looked up. Startled by her husband standing in the doorway, she didn't think for a second that her sudden abruption from the bed would awaken him, she just wanted to escape her dream that was beginning to turn into a nightmare. He walked over to her slowly and smoothed the hair from her face and looked at her long and tenderly. He knew something was wrong with her, but what? He wondered.

"Baby girl, what's going on with you, why are you out of bed?" He asked.

"I'm pregnant, I mean, I think I'm pregnant, I mean I think the universe, your God or something is trying to tell me I am!" She responded fearful and a little outraged. "And tonight, tonight I saw my mom and she was holding a baby girl!" She continued, her voice trembling.

"Honey wait, I don't understand, you're moving too fast" he said, mirroring the same expression she wore on her face. With her hand in his, he guided her over to the sofa, sat her down, and went to the refrigerator to pour her a glass of water.

Michael wanted to give her a moment to collect her thoughts. He walked back over to her, "Baby, you want to slowly explain to me what you're talking about?" He asked as he sat down beside her. She looked at him trying to gauge whether he was ready to know all about the reoccurring dreams and the baby, she knew it was now or never. She raised the glass to her lips and began to tell him all about the dreams in between sips.

"Okay, so I know we said we would never have kids," she muttered slowly, "but what if that's not the plan G--, God has for us," she said.

"Honey, what are you talking about?" he interrupted her quickly. He never interrupted her except for when he was nervous.

She looked down and continued, "That's what I'm trying to get to, the dream.... I've been having the same dream over and over and in it I'm pregnant with a baby girl. In this dream there is always a strong loving presence, I think it's, it might be, um, God or something like that," she said embarrassed. She continued, "And tonight my mother was in the dream and the baby," Vanessa said as she began to cry, "She was holding the baby and she looked up at me and smiled." She sobbed.

Michael took the glass of water from her hand and placed it on the coffee table. He laid himself back on the sofa and pulled her on top of him. Vanessa laid her head on his chest and sobbed softly. He knew that was all she could handle for the night, he didn't probe any further. He allowed her to cry as long she needed to while he held her. He lay there for a while deep in thought about what was revealed. What did it all mean? He thought. He gazed down at her, she had fallen asleep. He began to slowly let the sleep that was awaiting him take him in.

Chapter

4

ANSWERED PRAYER

She awoke swiftly as she heard her alarm ringing in the next room. The sun peaking in from their huge windows in the living room felt like it was standing on her face. She gazed up at her husband who was still asleep. *He must have been really tired*, she thought. She looked down and saw Diamond and Bentley looking up at her, she smiled. She took another glimpse at her husband and then remembered what she had told him the night before and the smile faded. *Why did I tell him? What must he think?* She wondered. She rose steadily trying not to wake him and to her surprise she was successful. He was usually a light sleeper. She grabbed the chenille blanket from the other couch and laid it on him.

Now in the restroom starring at the reflection that didn't look as familiar, she gasped. The luggage she was carrying under her eyes reminded her that she'd better get her full seven hours of beauty rest that night. Walking away from the mirror she went into her massive closet to decide what she was in the mood to wear that day. Carefully picking out each item with matching accessories, she decided that today had to be the day. She had to tell him everything. She scanned her brain for the best possible way and the light bulb went off.

Fully dressed, she peaked into the family room where Michael was still asleep then headed to the kitchen to make herself a small bagel and brew some coffee so that he could have some when he woke up. Wanting him to get some much needed rest, Vanessa called his office to inform his secretary that he would be late. He didn't have any court appearances until later in the day, so it worked out perfectly. It wasn't very often that he was late or even missed a day of work. If Vanessa didn't schedule his vacation time with his secretary and his partners he would never take it. He was passionate about all of the cases he took on and respected each of his clients like family. Before leaving she wrote him a note, it read:

Good Morning My Dearest Love,

Thank you for an amazing night last night! I know I've said this a million times before, but I don't ever want to miss the opportunity to tell you how grateful I am to be married to the most amazing, loving, caring, and giving man in the world! I know I must have shocked you with what I said last night and I would like to be able to talk with you some more about it. If you can get away from the office today, please make some time, I would love to have lunch with you at your favorite lunch spot around 1pm. I know you have a lot to do today, so I will make it brief.

By the way, you were sleeping so peaceful I decided not to wake you. I called your office and let them know you would be running late. There's fresh coffee waiting for you in the kitchen along with your morning paper.

I love you!

Your Breeze
~ V

Vanessa folded the letter in half and placed it on the coffee table in front of the sofa where he was sleeping. Outside the letter wore the impression of her sexy red lips where she had kissed it. She was sure seeing her lips on the outside of the letter would draw his attention. She kissed him on his forehead—he didn't even budge. *It's like he's in a trance, except for the fact that he's snoring*, she thought. She gave a quiet giggle and tip toed to the door.

Back at the office there was a lot to do, around 9:45am she received a text from Michael that read:

HEY BREEZE! I WISH YOU WOULD'VE WOKEN ME, I HAD SOME VERY CRAZY DREAMS. I'M NOT COMPLETELY SURE WHAT TO MAKE OF IT. I'LL SHARE IT WITH YOU WHEN WE MEET. (As not to alarm her too much about the dream, he changed the subject.) I LOVED MY SWEET LETTER YOU WROTE AND I LOOK FORWARD TO GAZING INTO THOSE LOVELY BROWN EYES OVER LUNCH. DO ME A FAVOR? COME TO THE RESTAURANT WITH NO PANTIES AND THOSE LONG STRIPPER BOOTS I LIKE?! :O)

Her response was what he had hoped it would be, she laughed when she finished reading the text. He always knew how to get a laugh out of her even through text. Michael knew her all too well, he was certain that if he hadn't lightened up the text with some fun humor she would've naturally focused on the dream and he didn't need her to worry; especially with her struggle with her own dreams. He needed to pray and seek God about what his dream meant and hers too; he was confident that they were connected and he needed clarity.

I will go into the office after I've met with Vanessa, he said within himself. He hadn't had a dream like that since God showed him that Vanessa was to be his wife. He called his office and gave his secretary specific instructions for his paralegal to handle for him while he was out. Michael concluded his call then proceeded into his prayer closet. He knelt down with his face to the ground, his bible open and he began to pray.

Before she knew it, it was noon. She begin finishing up what she was working on so she could meet her love on time, unlike Denise he was very punctual. Lucky for her the restaurant was only 10 minutes away from her job.

Emerging from his prayer closet a little after 12:15pm he felt refreshed and had clarity about his dream. He had lost track of time captivated in the atmosphere of prayer.

After glancing at the clock on the nightstand he realized he had to meet with his wife and didn't have much time to get ready. Still fellowshipping with the presence of the Lord that lingered within his spirit, he was at peace while still moving swiftly to get his suit on.

Even though he always stepped out looking like he had just finished a GQ magazine photo shoot, it never took him long to get ready. He was very easy on the eye, almost intimidatingly handsome, but his calm and caring demeanor quickly set people at ease. Stopping by the mirror for one more glimpse at all his handsomeness, he squirted himself a few times from the bottle of Clive Christian 1872, an expensive fragrance Vanessa had recently purchased for him for Christmas.

He looked at the clock, it read 1pm on the dot. He darted towards the door and decided he wanted to drive his sleek white 2015 Bentley Continental GT Convertible. The black Range Rover wouldn't be able to maneuver through traffic as easily. He was hoping to cut his 30 minute drive down 20 minutes, as not to make Vanessa wait too long. He loathed being late, although this time he was a pleased about the drive time, it would gave him more time to really settle into what he was about to share with his wife.

Vanessa pulled up to Oishī Japanese Cuisine right at 12:55pm and was shocked that she didn't notice any of her husband's cars in the parking lot. It was unlike him not to be at least 10 minutes early to a meeting. Just as she was getting ready to give her cell phone the command to call "Magic Man." That was Michael's assigned name in her contacts, she changed her mind. She considered the fact that something must've been really important so she decided not to pursue something that wasn't a big issue, besides she figured he'd fill her in upon his arrival.

Seated in a very cozy yet sexy area of the restaurant, she sipped her apricot tea, patiently waiting as she thumbed through the menu she already knew very well frontwards and backwards. On the verge of getting irritated she grabbed her phone from her purse, but before she could dial she felt her hair move to the side and a warm kiss planted to the back of her neck. With a smirk on her face, she knew who the kiss belonged to, she turned around and stood up to embrace her husband.

He pulled her in for a tight hug. Once he released her she held his face in her hands, pressed his lips into hers and kissed him. "Hey beautiful love, I'm so sorry I'm late. I'll tell you all about my morning shortly, first I want to get you fed. Let's place our order, I know you must be starving." Vanessa would get very loopy in her thinking if she hadn't eaten, she blamed it on the anemia that 'rudely invaded' (as she put it) her body several years ago. She usually followed a very strict eating time and at 1:37pm, it was well past that time. Since Michael was late and Vanessa always waited for him to order, he was right—she was starving.

"Okay baby." She said in a calm voice, "I'll call our waitress back over and order the usual." That was one of his favorite lunch spots, they were known by name and most of the wait staff knew their favorite meals. They made small talk as they waited for their food to arrive.

Not wanting to wait another minute she took a deep breath and on the last wave of air gliding from her lungs carried these words, "Ok, baby give me 15 uninterrupted minutes to finish the conversation I started last night." He usually never interrupted her, but she was fearful that what he was about to hear would cause him to prematurely end what she needed to finish.

Looking at her intently, he replied, "Sure honey" he sighed and continued, "I'm ready, but please before you start let me share with you a few things that I think will be helpful in what you want to share with me."

Totally perplexed by his statement, she responded, "Uh okay, baby, but I don't think you have a clue of what I need to tell you. But, sure proceed," she said impatiently as she motioned to him to continue.

"There's something I need to tell you, something you don't know about me." Immediately her thoughts went to, *oh no, an affair!* Then her mind calmly quieted itself and concluded with, *no, he would never cheat on me. He ain't crazy!* Vanessa clinched her fingers together under the table bracing herself, wondering what she could possibly not know about a man who knew everything about her.

Michael reached for both her hands. She hesitantly placed her hands in his. *That's a wise move. He wants to make sure I can't slap his face if he says something foolish!* She thought, trying to correct the grim resolution on her face. *Look pleasant Vanessa. He hasn't said anything yet. Stay calm and listen!* Hearing her thoughts she forced a smile on her face as she readied herself to hear some secret she didn't know about her husband.

Looking into the windows to her soul, he held her hands firmly, hoping she didn't slap him after she heard what he had to say. Michael continued, "Baby, for about three years now, I've asked God for a baby." She gasped. He could see the questions on her face. "I felt in my heart it was something you would never consent to so I never asked you, but I asked God to change your heart's desire and cause you to want a baby too. I wasn't sure if it was a prayer He would answer, so after about a year I gave up asking intensely and would only speak to God about it on days that the desire was unbearably strong, like when I would see family and friends with their children. In my disappointment I would even question God, wondering why He hadn't changed your heart."

He bowed his head and exhaled deeply—he felt terrible. He had broken a promise to his wife AND questioned God! They had promised to always tell each other everything, even their secret desires and wants. Now, for the very first time in all their married life, he betrayed their word to one another. He was ashamed!

Michael lifted his head gradually and located his wife's eyes again. "When you started talking to me about your dreams, I was fearful because it had taken so long I refused to believe that those dreams were my answered prayers. Not to mention I never asked Him to give you dreams about a baby, I asked him to change your heart. But, of course God never does things the way we think He should." He chuckled at the thought of God's unique methods and waited for her to chime in with a laugh or a smile, but when she didn't he continued, "But, last night I had a dream, Breeze. You were holding a beautiful baby girl and I was looking at you both and smiling. I was so excited and afraid at the same time! I needed to know that this dream was really of God, so I sought Him in prayer this morning, which is why I was late. After seeking Him, I have a peace in my spirit. I feel like it really is my answered prayer! He's changing your heart and confirming it to me through my dream.

He paused, it was a lot coming at her all at once. He wanted to give her a moment to take it all in. What he had to say next would probably be the most difficult of all had said.

Michael breathed deep, "Baby, it's time that we begin a new chapter in our lives by bringing a life into the world. I know this part is going to sound strange, but I believe through the life of this precious baby, God is going to provide some healing to your heart and help you release the pain of your mother's..." He stumbled over his words. "Your mother's death."

Vanessa was trying to hold in the tears as her eyes begin to burn. All at once the tears flowed out, spewing down her face onto her blouse and onto the table. He reached across the table and wiped the tears from her face with his dinner napkin. He sat patiently and waited for her to respond.

Vanessa was always a consistent, well planned person and it wasn't like her to up and change plans. She normally stuck to her decisions especially ones they had made as a couple, even if she wanted to, her 'stick to it nature' wouldn't allow it. He hoped after her dreams from God and what he said that her heart would be easily swayed. Even as important, he knew that this new season was going to bring some deep healing for his wife; another prayer that he had prayed to God for her over the years. He never thought God would combine the two, but God never does things the way we think He should, he thought.

She glanced at him and tried to regain her focus through her water-filled eyes. Vanessa eased right into her response to all he had said, "Okay, honey," she paused. "I'm on board. We can try for a baby."

He couldn't believe what his ears had heard, that seemed too easy. He reached across the table took her face in his hand and kissed her lips gently.

Still emotional, she attempted to compose herself to finish her response to him. "I was coming here to ask you if you wanted to start trying to have a baby and then you say all this and our dreams, I can't believe how similar they are. I even saw my mom in one of my dreams, she was holding the baby," she said trying to keep her voice from trembling.

Clearing her throat she continued, "Honey, I must admit I'm afraid, this whole thing seems so absurd to me! I mean I've never been one to be super spiritual or even one to have reoccurring dreams. And I'm an- angry at G-G-God! Why is He choosing to show up now and like this? Why after all these years?! My mom believed in Him right up until her death and He never healed her. She died! She died!" Vanessa screamed and immediately calmed herself as everyone in the restaurant turned their heads to look at them.

Michael looked at the people who looked at them and gave a reassuring smile that all was well. He realized his wife was finally dealing with many years of built up anger and pain. It hurt his heart, but he knew it was necessary. No one ever got better by ignoring things; it's only when they confront the pain and deal with it that they are able to heal, he rationalized in his head.

It was time for him to get her out of the restaurant and continue the conversation in a more private setting. Michael asked for the check, promptly paid for the meal they hardly touched and escorted his wife out of the restaurant. The valet brought her car to them, he opened the door and helped her get in the driver's seat. Once Michael got her settled he walked to the other side of the car and sat down in the passenger seat, he wanted to make sure his wife was okay. He looked over at Vanessa who was disheveled and was clearly shook up. He reached over to smooth the hair out of her eye and with the last stroke of hair from her face, she screamed from a deep place of agony within her. He had only seen her 'lose it' on two other occasions and one was when her mother passed away.

"Why, God why?" She yelled. "They call you a mysterious God, they got that damn right! You mysteriously let my mom die, she believed you, she loved you, lived for you, she taught me about you and she selflessly helped so many people...all for YOU! And how did you repay her?! You let her suffer and DIE!" She yelled pointing up, as she hurled accusations at her Creator.

"Now after all these years of being absent you want to come into my life and you and my husband want to convince me that a baby will magically make it all better! I watched her suffer. I watched as her hair fell out strand by strand, I watched her go from healthy to emaciated and frail! I witnessed her pain. I prayed with her, I believed with her and you didn't answer us GOD!" Why didn't you answer?! You said that by Jesus' stripes we are healed and yet you never healed my mother! You said You'd give us the desires of our hearts. I desired for my mother to live on earth with me, not leave me. I never knew my father, she was all I had and you took her from me! Now you want to give me something I have no desire for. When my husband prays you give him his desires, but not mine. I just don't understand!" She yelled as she sobbed more and more and louder and louder.

Once she finished her monologue Michael leaned over, pulled her as close as he could and held her. He could see she was in no position to drive and so he drove her home. Leaving his car at the restaurant was the least of his concerns, his only desire was to take care of his wife and make sure she was stable.

Vanessa was exhausted from crying. She felt like she had ran ten miles at full speed. He got her into the house and helped her get changed into comfortable lounge wear before helping her get into bed. Neither of them spoke a word, it wasn't time. Michael climbed in bed beside her, as she sobbed silently with her body facing the nightstand. He gently placed his hand on the small of her back and began to pray over her underneath his breath. Vanessa vanished in her emotional world and hadn't paid much attention to him praying for her. After he finished, he kissed her on the cheek and quietly exited the room.

Chapter

5

The GIFTER and HIS GIFTS

Michael returned to the kitchen to phone his office and hers to make arrangements with their staff for their absences. Then he called in a few favors with his friends to get his car home. Shortly after, he peeked into the room to check on her, only to find that she had fallen asleep.

Waking up startled and in a daze, reality hit her fast. She briefly looked at the clock on the nightstand, it read 7:18pm. She couldn't believe she had slept for over three hours. She sluggishly pulled her legs to the side of the bed to allow her feet to search for her slippers, immediately she felt something wet meet her toes.

"Well hello to you, sweet girl," she said, adding some cheer to her voice that she didn't really feel. Vanessa turned on the lamp that rested on the nightstand. She picked Diamond up in one hand with Bentley looking on wagging his tail. "Have you been there the whole time waiting for me, sweet girl? You love your mommy, don't you?" She said, realizing that saying the word mommy, now had a new meaning. She said it again, "Mommy, mommy, m-o-m-m-y." That word meant something different to her now that she accepted the possibility of becoming one. Still sitting on the side of the bed with Diamond on her lap and Bentley lying beside her, she sat quietly in a trance. The thought of being someone's mommy without having her own around to show her how—terrified her. Diamond licked Vanessa's hand and brought her back to consciousness. "What a perceptive little lady you are, you always rescue me from myself," she said with a warm smile, "Come, let's go check on daddy!"

Vanessa found Michael in the living room with his laptop on his lap handling business from home, a very familiar site. He welcomed her with a loving smile and motioned for her to sit down beside him on the couch.

"Baby, how do you feel?" He said touching her hand.

"Better, I feel much better, I'm sorry I...."

He interrupted her, "No need for apologizes baby," he said as he tucked her hair behind her ear. He continued, "Today was necessary for you, for us, I believe we are making a step in the right direction, God's direction."

"Honey, I'm still processing it all, I don't know....," he cut her off again.

"Breeze, I want you to continue on, but let me just say this first," he said.

"Okay, baby but, dang don't make this a habit. This is like the fourth time you've interrupted me while I was speaking, today." They both laughed because she only used slang expressions like 'dang' when she was extremely frustrated.

"This is the last time for the rest of our lives, I promise," he responded. They laughed again and he continued. "While you were sleeping I thought long and hard about what to say to you, what words I could choose that would comfort you and no words seemed befitting. Breeze, I know this has been a difficult few years for you and I'm so very sorry baby. I don't always understand why God does what He does, but I do know that He is a just God. There's one thing that life has taught me, through everything we must simply trust Him. He tells us that His ways are higher than ours and His thoughts are higher than ours. That means we may never understand why He does what He does. But, we can rest assured that all things no matter how bad they may seem, can and will work out for our good."

Seeing the hurt in his wife's eyes, Michael affectionately placed his hand on her leg. They both had enjoyed that they could tell each other difficult truths. He valued that she was the type of woman who could take it no matter how arduous. But, he wanted to provide her comfort as much as he could during those tough conversations.

Vanessa rested her hand on top of his. She appreciated his gentleness with her. He never belittled her or used harsh words. In moments like these, although he was her husband, she regarded him as a loving father because that was how he handled her, with a father's care.

"God promised to never leave us nor forsake us and baby while I watched you leave God, I watched Him never leave you. His hand has been so evident on your life; you've been so blessed, baby, and it's been God who's blessed you. He sent you someone that even though you lost your mom, you never had to go through the pain alone. I wanted nothing more than to carry your pain upon myself so you could be free. Watching you in agony has been one of the hardest things I've ever had to endure because I couldn't fix it, I couldn't take it away. But, I prayed for you every single day and night, some days my every prayer I prayed all day was for you."

He drew closer to her. Attempting to keep her tears locked securely behind her eyes Vanessa clung on to every word that proceeded out of his mouth. He continued, "You see while we are experiencing pain in this world, God is always there and if we'll look for Him, we will find him: in circumstances that He allowed to go our way, in the smile of stranger, in the prayers of a friend, or in the loving arms of someone who cares for us. Baby, all of that is God and my love for you and your love for me, is God. Your mom's love for you that got you to where you are today, is God! When we lose someone we love, our minds frantically search through all the whys and the what-ifs, looking for answers and coming up with nothing. But, honestly honey there are no answers to the questions that can stand up to the facts and the facts are, God blessed you with a great mother and even if she couldn't stay with you as long as you desired, you got to experience her life, grow in her love, learn from her wisdom and most importantly she gave you something so precious—she gave you God and God gave you the gift of her. We can't be mad when God comes to claim his gifts back to himself; they are gifts on borrowed time and eventually we will all be claimed back to the Gifter. But, if we appreciate and love each gift, when they're claimed back we can celebrate knowing they are now getting the best life has to offer in the Presence of the one that gifted us with a beautiful life here on earth, and an eternal home with Him in heaven. It's all a beautiful gift, baby, and that's why I'll never spend one day taking you for granted because you are my gift, just as your mom was yours!"

After what seemed like a closing argument in court, he was nervous to hear her response. This was the most he had ever said to her about her mother's death. He thought she'd have a lot to say, but to his surprise—she was speechless. She looked at him in silence for a few minutes as a few lonely tears strolled down her face. She was all cried out. He reached over to wipe the tears from her cheek. Vanessa pulled Michael's hand into her face and held it to her cheek as she rested her face in the palm of his hand, as she had done so many times with her mom during her final days. She would sit at the side of her bed and cuff her hand to her check. She smiled pleasantly at the thought of smelling it, examining it, every vein, and every line. She wanted the impression of her mother's hand forever engraved into her memory bank and it was.

"Thank you baby, all I can say is thank you," she said with his hand still pressed against her cheek. She released his hand from her face and pressed her lips into the palm it and for the first time in years she felt something that she hadn't known in years—she felt God. She could never accurately explain the feeling to others, but she knew what His Presence felt like. And right there in her living room, on her couch, with the love of her life, she knew He was there. She could feel Him resounding, vibrantly in her being. She looked up quickly, but said slowly, "Baby, do you feel that?" He simply smiled, he knew what she felt for he prayed for this moment many days and nights over the years. He recognized this was a special moment and he wouldn't dare cloud it with words. He just looked on with astonishment at his answered prayers.

Chapter

6

THE JOURNAL

Over the next few weeks it was touchy for her, she had really happy moments and moments where all she could do is cry. It was almost like she was grieving the loss of her mom all over again, however, this time it was the process of finally coming to terms with it all. God wasn't some evil tyrant who wanted to cause her deep pain and watch her suffer. He was actually good and loving and He loved her.

One evening Vanessa came home so exhausted from a busy day of work. She went to her room just to lie across the bed for a few seconds or so she thought. She fell into a deep coma-like sleep, still dressed in her work attire and heels. All of a sudden within her sleep state, she heard a faint bark, then it grew louder and louder, she startled awake to see Diamond looking up at her barking. She looked down at her wrist watch and noticed she had been asleep for almost two hours. "Oh my goodness!" She said rubbing her eyes. "Oh my precious babies, I'm so sorry my loves. You must be hungry, let me feed you."

Diamond and Bentley were so well behaved even in their hunger they would never jump on the bed uninvited. They had given their housekeeper some time off to take care of some family issues back home in Mexico, Vanessa hadn't been used to doing so much domestic work. She chuckled at herself, realizing that it had been quite fun for her cooking and taking care of all three of her babies.

She took her heels off and rolled out of bed, Diamond barked again. "Okay, okay, I'll feed you!" She followed Diamond and Bentley to the kitchen to prepare their food. Vanessa put fresh food and water in their bowls, just then she heard the text alert go off on her phone. She went to her purse that was still in her bedroom which was on the floor where she had left it. She never kept her purse on the floor, *I can't believe how tired I was*, she thought.

While searching through the purse her mom had gotten her for her 35th birthday, the year prior to her passing, her memory was triggered. "I had a dream," she said aloud. "I dreamt of her," she said to herself. The purse caused her to recall the dream. This time in the dream she saw her mother sitting in a rocking chair reading a book to the baby—her baby girl.

Immediately Vanessa dropped her purse and raced to the basement and down the stairs, she caught her breath as she reached the bottom of the stairs. Stopping at the end of the stairs her eyes frantically searched. *What area did she put my mom's things?* She wondered. "Maria!" She yelled up the stairs. "Maria!" She yelled again, no response. "What am I doing?" She questioned under her breath. She was in such a panic that she had quickly forgotten that Maria was gone.

Maria their housekeeper went home for a few months to be with her family after the passing of her father. It was an expense that Vanessa and Michael gladly took care of, even paying for her father's funeral. Maria had been with them for 10 years and had lived with them full-time after her Vanessa's mother had gotten sick. She had helped Vanessa take care of her and had been instrumental in helping Vanessa 'snap out of it' after months and months of intense grieving, where she couldn't even get out of bed or comb her own hair.

Maria was the one who took care of her when Michael was at work, she combed her hair for her and even on few occasion bathed her. Maria was more like family, like an older aunt to the both of them. As much as they were used to having her around they knew giving her paid time off and taking care of all her families' expenses was the least they could do after all she had done for them.

Vanessa plopped down on the bottom step and threw her head into her hands. Where do I began to look? She thought. Maria had everything so organized in their basement and Vanessa hardly ever went down there. She began to pray, "Okay God, I'm beginning to embrace all that you want for me and YOU, I'm embracing YOU again. Please let me know I'm not crazy, this book in my dream, I've seen it before, please help me find it. Uh....yeah, I think that's it for now. Amen!"

She rose from her seated position and walked over to what seemed to be endless shelves of organized containers. She looked closely and noticed they all had neatly typed labels on the side. Some read 'Michael's high school memorabilia', others had labels that read 'Vanessa's college books, and then she saw them, labels that read 'Betty's belongings'. Betty was her mother's name. She sighed in relief. Vanessa had a great appreciation for Maria's organizational skills. She walked over a few feet and grabbed the ladder, once it was positioned she begin to climb up four steps and on her tippy toes she rose to grab the first container. She pulled it down and went back for the next five containers with her mother's name written on the side.

Out of breath, she laughed at herself as she pulled down the last container. "Maybe Michael is right, I'm somewhat of a hoarder. Organized, but a hoarder none the less!" She said with a chuckle "I will certainly never admit that to him," she said amusingly.

She kept every single item that brought her loving memories of her childhood and her mother, however she knew that some items were not necessary, but she couldn't stand to part with them. Vanessa opened up the first box, she thumbed through old family photos and paintings that her mother had painted. She began to sob loudly. She saw her mother's favorite sweater, she put it up to her face and to her surprise it still had a faint scent of her mother's favorite perfume, Elizabeth Taylor's White Diamonds.

After meticulously going through the first three boxes she decided she'd better stay focused to find the book or she would be rummaging through her mother's things all night. Vanessa opened up the lids of two more boxes and realized that the book probably wasn't there. She sat down on the ground next to the box with her legs crossed, frustrated.

From her seated position she allowed her eyes to scan the book shelves. Her eyes moved from row to row, book shelf to book shelf, then there it was, the book! Her mother's journal. It was a beautiful royal purple. The cover was one her mother had decorated herself. She was very crafty.

Vanessa had watched her mother write in the beautiful purple book for months. However, her mother never wanted her to read it, "Not just yet," she would say in her customary soothing voice in response to Vanessa's inquires to read it. At times she would close it up the moment Vanessa walked into the room. As time went on and she grew weaker and weaker, Vanessa recalled her mother constantly reminding her to read the journal once she was gone. But, hearing her mother speak of her death was too painful of a thought subsequently anytime she spoke in that manner, Vanessa's mind automatically shut out what she was saying.

Vanessa grabbed the journal and pressed it against her heart as she walked back to her former seat on the bottom of the staircase. She cracked open the journal and begin to scan through the pages admiring her mother's beautiful handwriting she was never able to replicate. As a schoolteacher her mom had the fanciest handwriting and her mom always joked with her and called her writing chicken scratch. She caressed the pages thinking of the hours her mother must have spent pouring into page after page after page and now she was anxious to know what had she spent so much time writing about. There was so much writing in different colors of ink: black, blue, and her favorite color, purple. She went to the very first entry in the very beginning of the book and began to read.

My Journey Continues....

February 4, 2006

My Dearest Daughter,

I know it may feel like life has ended with me, but I can assure you my life, eternal life is just beginning and your life, well there's still so much to be lived. You still have life inside you and life to produce from you. I never wanted to scare you, but I knew the day would come where you and I would have to end our time here on earth. I just didn't know how to prepare you, and for that I'm sorry. I know this time has to be hard for you because we were all each other had for so many years. When you were a tiny girl I asked God to send someone who would love you the way you deserved to be loved and I thank God for answering my prayer.

Baby, don't be sad for me, I lived a beautiful life and you were the icing on the cake for me. You were more than I could have ever hoped for in a daughter and you were a miracle.

As you are aware I was never supposed to have kids, giving birth to you and watching you grow to the beautiful lady you are today reminds me every day that there is a God and that He is truly in love with us. I only pray that your baby girl will bring you as close to God as you have brought me to Him.

Life can be so mysterious we never know what moments become our defining moments, for me it was YOU. The day I found out I was pregnant with you was the day I gave my life to Christ and the day you were born was so magical I swear I heard angels singing.

Vanessa paused and laughed as tears strolled down her face, she had heard her mother tell that story so many times over her lifetime. She was so engaged in the love she felt spewing from the pages, she hadn't properly taken in the part where her mother wrote about her having a baby girl. She continued reading.

I'm not surprised who you grew to be, you were always a special sparkling gem in a world that at times seemed so unfair to you, yet you always found a way to sparkle and to shine. You have been my inspiration and my hope when I had none. It was your life that made me better. I'm so grateful that God allowed me to bring you into the world, your life caused me to LIVE!

Again I say, don't be sad for me for I have only transitioned to a different location and I can assure you that where I am today, I'm eternally happy.

There were things I wanted to say to you, to teach you, but my time ran thin. In the proceeding pages you will read those things! One thing I wish I would've prepared you for is motherhood. I know, I know you don't want any children, but that's not the plan God has for you. And as I've told you many times over, God's plans trump ours every single time! ☺ *Read my words, precious, with an open heart and mind! I AM PROUD of YOU Vanessa Monroe Morgan!*

I love you and I'm always with you, until we meet again.....LIVE! Mommy

Vanessa's eyes grew very big and began to mist again. She couldn't believe what she was reading. Her mom was always good at knowing things. Vanessa hardly ever got away with anything in her teen years, *but how could she have known this?* She questioned. The first time Vanessa had brought Michael to meet her mom, "She said thank you for finally introducing me to my son-in-law!" Vanessa sometimes thought she was crazy, but life always proved her to be right.

She closed the book gently. Her mother had always wrote her the sweetest, most impactful letters, but this had to have been the best one yet; her mother's final thoughts and words to her in her last few months of life.

Vanessa had always been the curious type. She found it peculiar that she had never taken an interest in looking for her mother's journal before. It had taken her seven years, several dreams, and a speech from her husband to even go looking for a book that she wasn't even sure she had in her possession. However, she knew the timing couldn't have been more perfect because she couldn't have handled reading it before now.

Chapter

7

"I'LL GIVE HIM WHAT HE WANTS!"

"Vanessa! Vanessa! Vanessaaaaa! Where are you?" She heard a familiar voice yell. She looked at Bentley and Diamond who had taken a nap at the top of the stairs while waiting for her. She hurdled up the stairs. *Why is there alarm in my husband's voice?* She wondered.

"Baby, I'm here! What's wrong?" She responded. They met each other at the top of the basement stairs.

"Babe, I texted you over three hours ago and when I didn't hear from you, I kept calling and calling and calling. I must've called 15 times in the last hour with no answer. I was worried. Are you okay?" He asked searching her with his eyes.

It dawned on her that he was the one who had texted her earlier. She had forgotten about the text and even the phone for that matter. She hadn't even realized that she had been in the basement a little over an hour. "Awe M & M, I'm so sorry. I was so drained I fell asleep the moment I got home only to wake up to a scavenger hunt!" She said with an inviting smile to put him at ease.

"Huh, wait a scavenger hunt? What kind of scavenger hunt?" He asked, now confused.

"Honey, it's a loonnngg story. Here, let's go to the kitchen while I find us something to eat and tell you all about it," she explained.

"Breeze, you need to rest, you've been cooking a lot lately, let me order us some pizza. Would you like some pizza?" Michael asked.

"Sure," she responded. Somewhat disappointed, she really liked making dinner now. Vanessa was pleasantly surprised at her newfound domestic skills. "On second thought just order me a salad."

"Baby, I can't eat a whole pizza by myself," he said.

She laughed and said, "Honey, order a small pizza."

"Come on, just eat one slice with me," he said with a sweet look on his face. They didn't eat pizza or greasy food often, so he really wanted to enjoy it and splurge. He had planned on eating most of it anyway, but he didn't want to seem too greedy.

She was aware of what he was up to. She said with a smile, "Okay, only for you I'll eat one slice, emphasis on one."

They both laughed. She was elated at how his presence had taken her out of the moment of everything that had just transpired. He called her Breeze, but he was actually her breath of fresh air. Just his "being there" could change her mood completely around.

She hadn't decided if she was actually going to eat a slice of pizza, but she reluctantly agreed to give him permission to order the size his heart desired. There were many times she said she would eat more than she actually did, it was their little inside joke. He knew what the outcome usually would be and so did she.

They made their way to the living room and sat down on the couch close to each other. She told him about the dream she had during her nap and finding her mother's journal. Vanessa opened up the pages and read a few journal entries to him. He could not believe what she was reading, "mother", was what he lovingly called her, knew one day a baby would be in their future. Just as she found a very interesting entry that was titled: 'The love of my life', the doorbell rang. It was the pizza guy.

Michael went to the kitchen to retrieve his wallet to pay the pizza guy while Vanessa got everything prepared for them to have a picnic style meal in front of the fire place. He was pleasantly surprised at her spontaneous and romantic thinking, she always kept him in remembrance of why he fell in love with her and why he remained there after so many years. He joined her, Bentley and Diamond who found their way to the picnic in front of the fire place with no fire. He brought the box of pizza along with Vanessa's salad over to the fancy black plush blanket and sat down beside her. This blanket had seen many sexy, romantic nights in front of the fireplace.

Michael glanced at the fireplace, "This is a great idea, I always love dinner in front of the fireplace, but baby there's no fire," he said jokingly.

She leaned over to him and glided her hand across his chest, "Baby, you know you're all the fire I need," she responded in fun topped off with a sexy smirk. He smiled big, revealing almost all his teeth.

Vanessa prepared their plates while Michael escorted Bentley and Diamond to their little room that Vanessa had created just for them some years ago against Michael's wishes. It had nice ceramic tile floors, all their fun doggy toys, a TV mounted on the wall because Vanessa was convinced they liked watching animal planet and little cubby spaces that housed their luxury custom made doggy beds. They'd much rather be close to Vanessa and Michael, but had been trained over the years to be satisfied in their room when escorted to go.

Michael wasn't sure how the night would end, but he thought he'd better be prepared in case it went out with a bang. To set the mood even further he went to the backyard to gather firewood to start a fire. Vanessa waited patiently thumbing through her mother's journal for the first 10 minutes, then as her stomach started to growl she was reminded that she'd better eat soon. "Baby!" She yelled in the direction of the backyard, "Are you almost done?" She asked. He hadn't heard Vanessa call his name. He entered in the living room shortly thereafter with fire wood in hand. When Michael entered the living room Vanessa smiled, she wasn't aware that he was getting firewood. Michael knew if he would have told her what he was doing she would've insisted he not do it.

"Baby, you shouldn't have," she said.

"Breeze, I wanted to," he responded endearingly. Her impromptu picnic by the fireplace planted thoughts in his head of 'dessert'. *I'll give him what he's wants; besides, I'm ovulating*, she thought, beaming. She had spent the last few days researching about ovulation and mapping out her own. It had been years since she had paid any attention to her cycle, she figured now was a good time to brush up. She hadn't wanted to tell Michael that she was ovulating in case she didn't get pregnant as she had hoped. *No one ever got pregnant the first time they tried anyway,* she reasoned, *we'll just see what happens*, she said within herself.

Michael ate his pizza, Vanessa ate her salad and a few bites of a slice of pizza. They chatted more about the journal. Michael was so impressed with what "mother" wrote, he read a few pages himself. As he was reading he noticed Vanessa starting to grab the plates and glasses of wine that they used for dinner. He put his hand on top of her hand, "Here, baby, let me," he said. He grabbed the plates from her hand, normally she would've objected, but she was fatigued.

"Awe thank you honey, you're so good to me," Vanessa responded as she leaned in to kiss him on the forehead. Michael proceeded to the kitchen with dishes in hand. Vanessa walked over to the couch to grab a pillow. She placed the pillow on top of the blanket and lay down in front of the warm fire that was sparkling brightly.

Meanwhile, in the kitchen she could hear Michael clanging the dishes around. *He must be rinsing off the dishes or putting them in the dishwasher*, she thought faintly as she watched the fire in awe. It was so mesmerizing to her, seeing the flames flicker back and forth as it licked up the life from the bark being burned up inside it. She began to settle more into her thoughts, thinking of the journal her mother had left behind and the baby. The warmth from the fire put her at ease as she began to dose off, she hardly notice the light in the living room go out.

Michael turned out the light when he returned to the living room. He closely watched her silhouette illuminated by the fire as he calmly approached her. She lay still anticipating his next move. He kneeled down beside her and pulled himself close into her, she felt his warmth on her back and his breath on her neck as he leaned in to kiss her behind her ear. Vanessa released a sigh as she reached behind her and caressed his head signaling to him that he was welcomed to take over. He gently rolled her over on her back, straddled her and descended down her body with soft kisses to her legs.

Michael reached up under her skirt to pull her panty hose down one leg at a time as he slowly undressed her, kissing her on her erotic zones, he could tell she was ready, but he wanted to indulge in the beauty of her body a little bit longer. He liked to tease her until she couldn't take anymore and would take over. She reached for him and they begin to kiss passionately as she rolled him over aggressively taking charge and ripping off his shirt. He loved when she got in the driver's seat and enjoyed the ride, no matter how bumpy. She looked at him fervently in the eye and then she devoured him in love making pleasure.

For weeks Michael and Vanessa were like newlyweds making love every chance they got and they made time for many chances. They'd always had a healthy sex life, but there was a new spark. They couldn't keep their hands off each other. They had decided they wanted to make baby making natural, they didn't want to partake in any of the ritualistic methods they had read and heard other couples try. They just simply wanted to make love, make love and make more love.

Chapter

8

<u>NEW FOUND HAPPINESS</u>

Vanessa was happier than she had been in a long time. With the help of her husband she had finally made peace with the loss of her mom and had even forgiven God. She now recognized His loving-kindness and goodness He had shown her over the years. A few weeks ago what started out as "just a friendly visit" to church with no promise of returning turned into an every Sunday and sometimes mid-week worship experience. Michael had a new light in his eyes. After praying for his wife for seven years, his prayers were answered. Vanessa came back to God! He was grateful that he never stopped believing even when it felt like the easiest thing to do.

One of the most incredible experiences for Michael happened during the mornings when Vanessa would wake up early and join him for prayer, she hardly ever missed a day of prayer until they started noticing something very different about Vanessa. Sleeping and eating became her new pastime. She struggled to wake up in the mornings and because of that she started to miss her morning prayer time with Michael. She even fell asleep at work every day after lunch.

After about the fourth week she supposed maybe her hormones were a bit off because she had dealt with some of the same issues a few years back and it was due to a hormonal imbalance. Vanessa was always energetic so the sudden changes she was experiencing alarmed her and Michael. Because they had never been pregnant before it hadn't dawned on either of them that the symptoms she was experiencing could be correlated with the changes a women experiences from being with child.

On a warm spring day Vanessa got up early to meet with her family doctor to find out what was happening with her body. She arrived 15 minutes before her appointment, signed in and sat down to answer the 'tedious' questionnaire. She wondered why she had to answer the same questionnaire she had already answered at least 50 times over the last 23 years. Vanessa had kept the same doctor since her sophomore year in college. She wrote in all her personal information, then moved to the portion that read: 'Your Medial History'. After answering all the invasive questions her eyes moved to the next section: 'Your Gynecological History'. The first question read: 'When was the first day of your last period?' Vanessa's eyes were locked in. She couldn't believe she hadn't noticed that her period was three weeks late. She had been in such a happy place in life coupled with so many new life experiences in God, enjoying an even more highly intense, passionate, romantic relationship with Michael and of course her always revolving busy lifestyle, it was no wonder it hadn't been missed. She admiringly looked down at her stomach, touched it tenderly, and smiled. She knew she was pregnant!

She filled in the blank space provided with the response: 'I'm three weeks late', next to it she drew a smiley face, then chuckled at herself. She was so absorbed in her new revelation she hadn't paid any attention to the lady next to her giving her a bizarre look. Vanessa looked over and smiled, but the older lady darted her eyes back to the TV. Vanessa smiled even bigger, *I'm sure she thinks I'm crazy*, Vanessa thought.

She transferred her eyes back to the questionnaire. The next question read: 'Is there a possibility you could be pregnant?' She didn't bother checking either box beside it that read: 'Yes' or 'No' instead she wrote in big letters: **'YES'** and smiled once again. This time she held back her laughter, she didn't want the 'old mean hag lady' as she called her in her head to give her the 'I wanna slap all 32 teeth out your head' look.

"Vanessa Morgan" she heard. She looked up and saw the nurse who greeted her with a warm smile. Vanessa got up and walked over to her, she returned the smile and gave her the clip board. She followed the nurse back to the examining room in a robotic state. Vanessa had been talking and answering the nurse's questions, but not fully present. She now knew why she was there and couldn't wait for it to be confirmed. The nurse asked her to get on the scale, she looked at Vanessa in shock, "Vanessa you're almost at your goal weight, you've gained 11 pounds," her nurse said.

Vanessa's nurse had been at her doctor's office for almost as long as she had been a patient. She was Vanessa's doctor's wife and they were good friends of some of Michael's good friends, so she knew Vanessa's health history pretty well.

Vanessa looked over at Margo and blurted out, "I'm 113 pounds, no way, I must be pregnant. Wait, this can't be good, right I've gained so much weight so fast." She looked at Margo puzzled.

"Wait a second, you think you might be pregnant?" She asked excited. "Oh no, you guys didn't want any kids, right?" Her voice changed, she didn't know if she should be happy or sad for Vanessa.

Vanessa, consumed in her excitement, reached over and hugged Margo. "We didn't want kids, but we do now!" She said releasing her enthusiastic filled words.

Margo was in total shock. Vanessa was never that friendly and to go as far as to give her a hug, they had never hugged before! Vanessa was always so sterile and very business-like when she came in for a checkup. There was a new and refreshing vibe about her. Margo didn't want Vanessa to sense her uneasiness with Vanessa's new persona. Margo calmly smoothed her clothes back into place, attempting to gather herself. She looked down at the clip board and read what Vanessa wrote on the questionnaire. Margo smiled at Vanessa and said, "I think you just might be right; we'll do a pregnancy test while you wait for Doctor Stern."

Margo had Vanessa go into the restroom, pee in a cup and leave the specimen for her to retrieve and test. Meanwhile, she proceeded with all the other necessary procedures; she checked her blood pressure and heart rate. When Dr. Stern arrived Margo stepped out to test her urine. The whole time Vanessa was talking to Dr. Stern, all she could think about was the test results and telling her husband the wonderful news.

When Margo walked in it felt like everything in the room stopped, the only action that grabbed Vanessa's attention was Margo gradually approaching her hospital bed. It seemed that each step took forever. Vanessa turned to look at Margo, but she gave a polite smile and diverted her attention back to her husband who was talking about, only God knew because Vanessa was clueless. They were engaged in small talk about their mutual friends they shared. Well, he was deep in conversation, she was just listening or pretending to and would give the occasional, "uh huh" and "really", hoping he would think she was engaged and hurry up. Vanessa was on the verge of telling him to shut up and let Margo speak, but she quickly realized that wouldn't be a wise move. She hoped Margo would interrupt him, although she was very clear that that would have been a disastrous move too, not to mention it would've been just plan rude.

Margo waited patiently for another five minutes as she kindly smiled and nodded in agreement at every word he said. He loved to talk. He saw his wife standing close by, but didn't acknowledge her presence. It was like he had forgotten why Vanessa was there and that she was waiting for some very life altering information. Vanessa decided she didn't want to wait any longer, she blurted out, "So what are my results?" Dr. Stern directed his attention to Vanessa, bothered that she would interrupt him.

Dr. Stern was one of the top physicians in the region and that was the only reason Vanessa continued to allow him to be her doctor. Now nervous but anxious, Vanessa waited for Margo to speak.

"You're pregnant!" Margo said with joy. Immediately Vanessa began to cry, she knew now more than ever God was real.

"Are you okay?" Dr. Stern asked.

"Yes, yes I'm fine, it all has happened so fast." Vanessa responded trying to regain her composure.

This was a side of Vanessa Dr. Stern and Margo had never seen before. She asked them to give her a moment alone to get her clothes on and let the news settle in. They weren't sure if they should leave her alone, but she reassured them that she was really happy and that her tears where tears of joy. They stepped out and left Vanessa alone with her thoughts. *Who knew two simple words could make me so happy.* "You're pregnant"' those two words would forever change her life and she was so glad she allowed what was connected to her life to now exist in her life. As she lay back on the hospital bed still wearing the patient robe they had given her, she reflected on the numerous situations that brought her to this very place in her life. She pictured her mom in the room with her smiling with pride. Vanessa smiled and touched her belly once again as she began to dress herself.

She emerged from the patient room 20 minutes after Dr. Stern and Margo left, fully clothed and headed to the clerk to make her co-payment, Margo came over to check on her.

"Vanessa. How are you feeling? Are you okay? Should I walk you to your car?" Margo asked.

"Yes, I'm okay, I'm more than okay, I'm great actually, "She said as she kindly touched Margo's arm to reinforce that she really was okay. "I'll be fine walking to my car, thank you for offering! You and Dr. Stern have been so great," Vanessa concluded. She was reminded of why she stayed with Dr. Stern, even though he could be bothersome at times with all his talking and arrogance, they were caring and actually concerned about her total well-being.

This time Margo welcomed the warm vibe Vanessa was putting out and she pulled Vanessa in to give her a hug. "Well, congratulations, Dr. Stern and I couldn't be happier for you and Michael. We'll keep tight lipped about it. I can't wait to hear the news circulating and everyone's excitement for you. We are so thrilled to be seeing more of you in the coming months! Your next appointment in four weeks will be your first official prenatal check-up!"

Vanessa smiled, she hadn't thought about the whole process of being pregnant and what her new lifestyle would be like. Margo handed her a bag full of information and goodies concerning her next several months as a pregnant woman.

"Oh thank you Margo, I can't wait to tell Michael," she said. She finished all her business at the doctor's office and headed to her car. She slid down in her seat and began to thank God, "God, I have to be one of your top five most difficult children!" She said as she released a hearty laugh. I just want to take some time to say thank you! Thank you for blessing me with the opportunity to be a mother! Thank you for giving me eyes to see what I couldn't see for myself! Thank you for still loving me when I had walked away from you and was so unlovable! And God, thank you for letting me know that my mom is still with me in my heart and watching over me as my guardian angel!

Oh my God" she screamed, "I'm going to be a mother! Thank you, thank you, thank you Father God! I must admit I'm scared, but if *You* trust me, I trust me," she said confidently.

She hadn't quite figured out how she was going to tell Michael, she started her car and gave her phone car system the command, "Call Magic Man." The phone rang once and then she hung up. *No, that's not how I want to tell him,* she thought. She hoped he was too busy to notice her call and wouldn't phone her back. She began brainstorming. *Maybe I'll take him to lunch*, she thought. *No, I'll put a note in a gift box that says I'm pregnant and present it to him when he gets home tonight.* The wheels in her head continued to churn. *No, no, I'll have a dancing baby telegram sent,* she chuckled at thought of some grown person dressed as a baby and singing. She cringed. *Oh that's a horrible idea!* She sat quietly rummaging through her thoughts for several more minutes, "Oh I got it! That'll be perfect!" She said aloud to herself.

She called Cindy to let her know that she would be out the rest of the day, but would come in bright and early the next day. Cindy was good at handling things while Vanessa was away and she was exceptionally glad she took the day off because lately Vanessa had been so abnormally cranky at work. Vanessa hung up quickly. She was so excited. She knew if she stayed on the phone too long she wouldn't have been able to contain the good news. She made a quick run to get groceries to prep for her plans to tell her husband the wonderful news.

Vanessa burst through the door with enthusiasm and headed straight for the kitchen humming a little tune her mother hummed when she was happy. Bentley and Diamond were waiting at the door with their tails wagging when she walked in. "Hello my babies! Let me get started on the special plans I have for daddy tonight and then I'll feed you, "she said with a gigantic smile.

She went into the kitchen and began preparing dinner for her husband. She bought T-bone steaks, red potatoes and asparagus. She had a special treat that would help reveal her surprising news. She was so ecstatic she could hardly contain herself! Vanessa sung the whole time.

Making her final touches to dinner, she worked diligently on her special surprise. With everything complete she stood back in admiration, eyeing what she had created, she was proud of her handiwork. She had nibbled a few bites and her tongue danced and leaped in her mouth. She was a great cook and Michael was going to love her meal! The saying was true, the quickest way to a man's heart was through his stomach and boy did she know how to speak his stomach's language.

All at once the exhaustion of the day had caught up with her, she needed a hot shower to relax her and prepare herself for her husband's coming. She texted him to make sure he was still getting off early like they had talked about the day before. Since he couldn't make the appointment with her because he had to be in court that morning he wanted to spend the evening with her to redeem himself for his absence. It wasn't anything she required, but it was how he was postured towards her. He cherished being her support, especially in moments like these, but when he couldn't he always found a way to make it up.

He texted her back: YES, MY LOVE, I SHOULD BE HOME AROUND 5:45!

She put the phone down, noticing the time on her phone read 5:03. She took her clothes off, and headed for the shower.

She invited the warm water to glide down her spine as she relaxed into herself. With all the excitement of the day, she hadn't realized how much anxiety was bound up in her body. She took a deep breath and released it. Vanessa allowed her thoughts to scan through the day and she became overwhelmed with gratitude once again, tears of happiness strolled down her face. She had lived a very accomplished and successful life, but on the inside she used to be so broken and angry at life after her mother's passing. She now found herself in a place she would've never imagined—no longer bitter at God, in fact she was back in love Him AND PREGNANT. She looked up and said a very faint, "Thank you."

As she released her gratitude into the atmosphere more tears began to stream down her cheeks. What started out as a shower turned into a worship session. She worshipped God and thanked Him! It felt foreign hearing the words come out of her mouth, "I love you Lord! You're so awesome! Thank you for looking past my hurt, my anger, and still deciding you would bless me, you would love imperfect me! Thank you, I know I'm not worthy and yet you're so faithful! Thank you for loving me," she said as she held herself up against the shower wall now sobbing.

What sounded strange quickly became familiar. She had heard her husband over the years in the shower, in his prayer closet, in the kitchen, in the restroom, at work, in their bedroom and even out in public worshipping and thanking God. He was never shy or afraid of displaying his love for God wherever he went. He often told people God was a part of him and when people saw him they saw God!

She had heard her mom on many, many occasions worshipping and thanking God even on her sick bed. Then it emerged to her memory: she remembered how she used to worship God. It had been so many years that she had forgotten. She found her beautiful words of worship unto her God and she felt more at peace than ever. It was like she was home in herself once again.

Vanessa stepped out of the shower feeling refreshed and ready to share a terrific evening with the love of her life. She put on her beautiful, sexy negligee, but before she did she wrote something on her stomach with a black marker. She giggled. It was more difficult than she had suspected to write legibly on her stomach. She had washed her face in the shower so all that was left to do was add a small amount of tinted pink lip gloss, she didn't want much lip action just a little shimmer. She put on her pearl earrings that went perfectly with her long white flowing negligee. Vanessa pulled her hair up in a bun just in time to hear the door chime from their home alarm, signaling Michael had arrived.

Vanessa rushed out quickly to greet him. Before he could get through the door she grabbed his suitcase and took off his suit jacket. She hung his coat up on the coat rack then guided him to the living room, Vanessa kneeled down in front of him and gently removed his feet from his shoes. Then she added her greeting's final touch, a warm, slow, soft kiss on his lips. Michael felt mighty kingly! Vanessa loved to serve her man as she did often. He had a rough day in court and her extra tender care was exactly what the doctor ordered!

"Thank you, baby." He said in a low relaxed tone. She could tell by his tone that he was tired, however she maintained her excitement. She wanted to rush to the kitchen, make his plate and get dinner started already, so they could get to the dessert. But she knew it was best that she maintain her composure.

"You're welcome, love!" Vanessa responded. She kissed him on top of his head and sat on his lap. "Let me get a good look at you," she said as she looked him deep in his eyes. "Awe, baby I can tell you had a tough day," she continued. "Well, I made you dinner, your favorite steak, red potatoes and asparagus AND I have a little surprise for you after dinner!" She said as she rubbed his hair.

He kissed her on the lips, "Oh you do, do you?" He had been so fatigued it took him a moment to rest into his home surroundings and SEE her. It was a rare that he was that distracted with the stress from work, but it did occasionally happen.

Finally looking into her eyes, he was drawn in. "Oh honey, you look sexy," he said perking up a bit. She had become so accustomed to what he liked that she seldom ever wore PJ's to bed unless her unfriendly visitor was around, the one that came once a month and brought all types of chaos with her. He knew this night could go two ways either, making love or not making love and he was hoping for the first.

"Thank you, babe! Listen, put your feet up, relax, I'm going to get your plate ready. I'll come back to get you when it's ready. Relax," she said again as she rubbed his shoulders for a few seconds. She finished the impromptu massage and disappeared into the kitchen. After about ten minutes, she reappeared only to find her dinner date snoring. Normally she would've let him rest, but she had something to share and he needed to hear. She lightly nudged him on the shoulder a few times, after that didn't work, she stood over him and slowly pressed his lips against hers. That usually woke him up. Just as anticipated, he woke and acted like he was never asleep.

"Oh hey, baby," he said slowly and rubbing his eyes. "What are you doing?" He said with a smirk as he playfully pulled her in to sit on top of him.

"Oh nothing just trying to wake you up, my love!" She responded sarcastically then laughed. Vanessa always thought it was funny when he acted as if he wasn't asleep, she knew what his next reply would be.

"What! Sleep?! Who me? Girrrlll! You know your man don't sleep!" Michael said with a wink.

"Yeah right! Get up baby! Come with me so I can feed my man who never sleeps!" She planted another kiss on him then pulled him up by the arm. He smacked her butt as she walked away. Vanessa turned around, "Baabbyy!"

Michael smiled, "What----what did I do? That was Bentley!" He looked down at Bentley who was closely following behind Diamond who was right on Vanessa's heels.

"Bentley, you betta keep your hands off my woman! Diamond, get your man and go lie down!" He said. Bentley and Diamond looked up at Michael puzzled and Vanessa and Michael looked at each other and laughed.

"You are silly! What shall I ever do with you?!" She said jokingly.

"Well that's easy, love me of course, feed me good meals, and love me up until my toes curl. See, baby, I don't ask for much! I'm a simple man!" He said laughing at his own little dirty joke.

Michael reached for her hand and twirled Vanessa around, now facing the back of her, he pressed his chest against her back, cradling his arms around her, and doing a slow wind dance motion while kissing her ear.

She laughed, releasing herself from his grip of love, "Uh huh, behave it's not time for all that right now. Seriously babe, I want to feed you."

He sensed her determination to keep him focused, he relented "Okay, okay, let's eat and we can handle the last item on my list of simple man needs after dinner!"

Vanessa didn't respond, she simply pointed to the table for him to sit down in front of his plate she had already prepared. They shared small talk about their day. Michael noticed Vanessa was eating faster than usual, but didn't want to make a big deal of it. He had observed that she had picked up a few pounds, but he didn't mind it and he certainly didn't want to make her feel self-conscious about her new found love for big portion sizes, greasy foods, a cupcake almost every day, pickles, and chocolate milk shakes from McDonald's all of which she would've never even lifted to her lips weeks before.

Vanessa was eating fast on purpose, she was extremely hungry, but more than anything she wanted to get through dinner so they could get to the surprise. She finished up her food while Michael was still eating. She hurried him, "Baby you're eating so slowly. Can I have a bite of your red potatoes and steak?" She asked.

"Um, honey, you want a bite of my red potatoes AND steak?" Vanessa gave him a strange look. "Okay, yeah, sure! Take as much as you like." Michael stated, but it was more of a disguised question.

She reached over and gobbled two big bites, Michael tried not to laugh. "Here baby, let me wipe your mouth," he said as he extended his arm towards her mouth with his napkin in hand. Before he could wipe her mouth she licked the A1 steak sauce residue from the corner of her lips. He slowly withdrew the napkin back to his lap. He could no longer hide his amusement, a smirk escaped his lips.

"What, baby? What's the smile about?" Vanessa asked puzzled.

"Um, well," he didn't really want to answer and he didn't want to lie either. "Well my precious," he continued with a pause, "your appetite seems really ravenous tonight. Honey, did you eat today?" He saw the peculiar look Vanessa was giving, he knew he should've kept his mouth shut. He figured he'd better recover the situation or he was going to regret it really soon if he gave her time to respond. "Doesn't matter to me, you know I find a greedy woman sexy. Save that appetite for later, I want to be ravished!" He said giving her his sexy, funny face. It was the face he gave when he was simulating his sexy expression while wanting to make her laugh.

Vanessa looked at him for about 15 seconds, she wasn't sure whether to laugh or be upset. She tried to decipher whether he was giving her compliment or not. He always said stupid stuff when he was trying to defuse perceived tense. She obliged him with a little giggle, after all she knew why she was eating more. He forced out a giggle with her, he was just glad it didn't go bad.

"Baby, finish up and hurry! I have some dessert I think you'll like," she persisted as she moved away from the table heading towards the kitchen.

He was talking to her from the dining room as he continued to eat. "Baby, I'm telling you I think Judge Brown has it in for me, she always gives me such a hard time. I'm really praying tomorrow goes better. After dinner will you pray in agreement with me concerning this? I really need God to give me favor with her. Wait a second." Michael halted his conversation abruptly recalling that she had a doctor's appointment earlier that day. Today had been so intense that he had forgotten all about it and had even forgotten that that was the purpose he had come home early.

Right when Michael was about to ask her about the appointment, he looked up from his plate and there stood the love of his life. There was something almost magical about her standing there in that moment. His eyes were fastened to hers and hers to his. He looked down and saw that she was holding something—her glass cake plate. He watched her meticulously as she brought it closer to him and set the cake plate on the table in front of him. They both held their unbroken gaze fixed on one another.

There was something so different about her energy and he couldn't quit put his finger on it, but it was electrifying. He sat anxiously anticipating her next move!

Vanessa broke the silence with, "My love I have a surprise for you!" She said excitedly as she removed the dome from the cake plate. It was a heart shaped cake that read, 'Hi Daddy'. He looked up at her perplexed. She called him daddy, but only during love making. She opened her long sheer robe that was a part of her negligee, then removed the veil that was covering up her stomach. She looked down smiling with her hands on her hips drawing Michael's attention to her tummy that read, 'We're Pregnant!' written in red marker. Michael's eyes filled up with tears. He picked her up and spun her around. Her legs straddled across his waist and her arms clung tightly around him as she tucked her face into his neck. When he attempted to put her back down her legs stayed wrapped tight.

She loved when he picked her up; being held in his massive arms, she felt like a tiny girl, so vulnerable and yet so safe and secure. This was a man who had loved her without conditions; he loved her back to life, back to herself. God used him to revive her. Since her resurrection back to what she called "lively living", she often wondered how she had lived so long disconnected from the Vine of life.

He looked Vanessa deep in her eyes and their souls became reacquainted. They were overcome with a deep passion—the kind that seem to shut the world out and lock them inside a world where only the two of them existed. Enveloped in his love, she kissed him.

Still gripping her tightly he carefully walked her into the kitchen and sat her on the large island. Michael pulled back the sheer robe and the strap to Vanessa's negligee, revealing her bare shoulder, he began to kiss it tenderly. They knew exactly what this exchange of love meant and he too basked in her love. She caressed his head then grabbed onto him tightly as they kissed. Bentley and Diamond looked up at their parents, a scene that wasn't unfamiliar. Diamond held her head low and exited out of the kitchen with Bentley following close behind.

Chapter

9

<u>HISTORY OF LOVE</u>

Michael was in a deep coma-like sleep accompanied with mild snoring. After a long day and a full intense hour of love making, he was exhausted. Vanessa lie in bed next to the man that completed her heart, reflecting on the history of their love. When they made love it was like their souls intertwined, they connected soul to soul and spirit to spirit. She knew what they shared was rare and many people would never get the opportunity to taste the brand of love they experienced. Theirs was a unique love that had held an anchor in the ground even when the world around them was quaking.

They shared great times, happy moments, and some very lowest of the lowest, horrifying times. When asked how their marriage withstood so many challenges of life, her answer was always, "I married my best friend, our friendship has always been more important than our marriage because if the friendship is healthy then the marriage part is a <u>Breeze</u>!" (Which was one of the reasons

Michael had given her that name.) It was their friendship that bound them together and their commitment to their friendship that had given their relationship longevity throughout the years.

They had experienced their first fight nine months into their marriage and it looked like they weren't going to make it. Vanessa fled and went to stay with her mom for three days. It was after the separation that they both realized they needed to be in each other's world, they vowed to never speak of the word divorce again, and they never did. They understood they were much better together than apart. Since they had a wonderful friendship before marriage, they pledged to define their marriage based on their friendship and not based on the roles of marriage that society had set. They both had quirky and eccentric parts to their personality, but it was something they understood about each other and accepted each other unconditionally.

Michael moved a little closer to Vanessa and she grabbed his arm and wrapped herself up in him, spooning her body, one with his. *How many people could sleep like this?* She wondered. They did many nights. He was her security and protection and she was his tranquility and stability. For the first time in a long time everything felt right in her world, snuggled tightly in his arms, eventually she drifted from the thought world to the dream one.

Chapter

10

<u>MY DEAREST DAUGHTER</u>

The final day of her pregnancy had arrived. Vanessa was nervous. She had so many emotions welling up on the inside of her. It had been a great nine months; despite her age everything had gone well. It seemed as though it had gone fast, she and Michael cherished every moment of it. She might have enjoyed it a little too much, she had gained 48 pounds and made no apologizes for it. She ate what she wanted when she wanted until she started to swell too much then her doctor advised her to cut back on the salty foods. She still walked moderately, but she relished in her newfound curves. She particularly treasured the fullness she carried in her breasts, Michael especially loved it and indulged in all the beauty of it.

It was 5:45 AM, Vanessa and Michael were getting checked in to St. John's Medical Center on the 7th floor of the maternity ward in Atlanta, GA. They found out the confirmation of what they were having early on in her pregnancy. Armed with their pink car seat, pink

Petunia Pickle Bottom diaper bag full of diapers, wipes, pacifiers, a few very pink cute outfits with ruffles and matching bows, bottles and her breast pump—they were ready to go. In her large Louis Vuitton bag she had all her essentials including a very luxurious gown and a plush pink robe that she planned to wear after giving birth. There would be lots of visitors and she didn't want to look like she had just been hit by a train even if she might've felt like it.

She read many books on pregnancy, childbirth and being a first time mother. Vanessa had taken all the child birthing classes she could think of, she wanted to be armed with as much information as possible. Her pregnancy had gone two weeks over her due date, therefore she was able to schedule her delivery date and be induced. Vanessa was actually quite glad; the one thing she was nervous about was going into labor and not getting to the hospital in time for the baby to be delivered.

Vanessa and her husband where escorted to their delivery suite where they would be staying for the next few days. She was overwhelmed with enthusiasm when she entered the room Michael and Cindy had custom designed to her liking for her brief stay there. Michael had her room filled with a few dozen red, white and yellow roses, her favorite flower. Because she was an interior designer she loved being in environments that where pleasing to the eye and gave off a welcoming vibe. They even had her favorite sushi and a few of her other favorite snacks housed in the tiny refrigerator in her delivery room ready for her to eat after she gave birth. Michael was aware of her nervousness and wanted to do as much as possible to put her at ease, even spending big dollars to make her stay more comfortable. The hospital staff was nice and her doctor had been great. There was nothing more she could have asked for.

They got settled in and Michael got out his camera to set up. His mom would be arriving soon and she was going to tape the whole thing. There was no way they were going to pass up capturing a moment that would live in the history of their lives forever. She glanced over at her Louis Vuitton bag and saw her mother's purple journal tucked away in a side pocket. Reading the journal had become customary over the last several months; many pages she read over and over. She was looking forward to reading the one titled 'Now that you're a Mommy!' In the margin her mother wrote, 'Please wait to read this section once your life has produced a life, your child, my grand-baby. Vanessa was always one to honor her mother's wishes and as anxious as she was she waited.

Hours had passed, Vanessa had been induced and had received her epidural. She had only dilated to a five, this part she thought would go quicker. Cindy, Denise, Michael's parents, his brother, his sister and their families had joined in the waiting game. They were all excited to meet the new addition to Vanessa's and Michael's life. The next few hours passed quickly as Vanessa had intense contractions, many she didn't feel because she was so heavily sedated. She went in and out of sleep, talking and laughing with everyone around her then falling back into a deep sleep only to be awakened every hour by nurses who were checking her vital signs and seeing how far she dilated. After the eleventh hour of being in labor it was the big moment, she had dilated to a 10 and it was game time. It only took her seven hard pushes and she heard the most joyous sound. A faint squeaky, shriek of a cry as tears flowed from her and Michael's eyes, his mother's and even their nurse, Margo cried.

It was such a beautiful and magical moment. When Vanessa looked into her precious baby's eyes, she instantly fell in love. She and Michael had decided to wait until the baby was born to name her; the moment she looked at her she knew her name had to be Faith Ann Morgan. Faith, because it was her life that was a part of the process of bringing back Vanessa's faith; and Ann, because that was her mother's middle name. It was such a joyous occasion, she had birthed Faith, but Faith had birthed her too!

Vanessa was trying to settle in to her new role as mother, but everything was happening at the speed of light—painful attempts at breastfeeding, visitors, nurses, checkups, changing diapers, and trying to keep some sense of normalcy in the midst of chaos just didn't exist. Vanessa, being a girl who's used to order, it was a little exasperating for her. Michael, her calm guardian was by her side to navigate the hustle and bustle of the day.

As night approached and visitors began to wane, Michael knew just the thing to help Vanessa relax. Vanessa had just made a major accomplishment, it was the night feeding for Faith and after trying all day with little success, it happened! Vanessa was able to get Faith latched on and achieved her first successful feeding! Vanessa was feeling tired, but she wanted to keep Faith in the room with them. She was nestled in the bed holding Faith. Vanessa had shared with Michael that her mother had written a special letter to be read once she had given birth and he wanted to have the pleasure of reading it to Vanessa. He walked over to the Louis Vuitton bag and grabbed the purple journal and walked back to the bed with journal in hand. He smoothed the hair from Vanessa's eyes and kissed her forehead, he was so proud of her. Michael sat on the side of the bed, looking proudly at his beautiful baby girl. What a sight to behold, he thought.

He leaned in and kissed Faith on the top of her head, she was sleeping peacefully in her mother's arms.

Michael looked Vanessa deeply in her eyes, still holding the journal. That was his way of communicating his desire to read the letter she had been anticipating all these months. They had shared many conversations merely with their facial expressions, eyes and body language. That's one of the things he loved most about her, she was his soul mate and their connection ran deep. She nodded in agreement for him to proceed. Vanessa sank deeper in bed and looked down at her baby girl as he thumbed the pages to find the entry that was already bookmarked. Michael cleared his throat and began to read:

Now that you're a Mommy!

March 30, 2006

My Dearest Daughter,

Today is one of most beautiful days of your life! Take the time to breathe in everything that today is and all that it means, soak it all up like a sponge. While it's a day that you and Michael will never forget, it is also a day that is moving fast from your present and soon will be in your past, so relish each moment. Take in her smell, her first smile, the way she gazes into your eyes, the way she studies your every feature and if she is anything like you she will watch you very carefully. ☺ I know you have so many questions and doubts. You will do great! Take confidence in knowing that you are equipped and built for this!

I remember one time when you were about four or five years old and I had bought you this baby doll. You loved that doll like it was your real baby. You held her all the time, changed her clothes, and you even convinced me to buy her some diapers because you said you didn't want her to get pee on her clothes.

One day you went to visit Aunt Sheila and I persuaded, no I bribed you to leave the baby doll home. It was with great reluctance that you left her home on your bed. I cleaned your room and moved the doll to the shelf with all your other baby dolls, in my mind it was just another toy. When you got home you ran straight to your room to look for that baby doll and when you didn't see her on the bed your knees buckled under you and you clasped to the ground sobbing deeply. I asked, Vanessa what's wrong baby? You said someone kidnapped my baby. I didn't even know where you had gotten such an idea, but you were certain of it.

I picked you up off the ground and I walked you over to the shelf where I had placed your baby doll. You grabbed her from the shelf, pulled her close into you and you held her in your arms. I knew that very moment that one day you would be one of the most amazing mothers.

I have faith in you baby! Give yourself permission to be imperfect, mistakes are inevitable so don't be afraid of them, it's a part of living, learning, and growing. Whenever you have doubts, tap into the Holy Spirit and the deep wisdom that rest on the inside of you. You have a rare kind of love Vanessa, spill it into everything you do and say with your daughter and you can't fail because Love always wins, it never fails. Enjoy the ride of motherhood, you are in some of the most amazing times of your life!

I love you eternally,
Mommy

Michael finished reading and looked up at Vanessa's tear-stained eyes, he pressed his cheek against her wet face absorbing some of her tears into his skin and then gently wiped the rest away with the back of his finger. Michael kissed her on the cheek and took the baby from her so she could rest. He sat down on the couch with Faith swaddled in his arms; he wanted to give Vanessa some time to let the words her mother wrote soak in.

A few weeks had passed and Vanessa was still home on maternity leave. She was beginning to establish a routine more and more each day. It had been a crazy and abrupt interruption into their lives, but very welcomed and even necessary for her to begin the next chapter of her life. She had just fed Faith and put her down for a nap; she was amazed at what a great baby she was. A few weeks before Vanessa had Faith, she had purchased her own purple journal and decided today would be her first entry. Vanessa sat down in the rocker in Faith's nursery with the journal and pen in hand and she began to write.

The Introduction!

June 23, 2014

My Dearest Daughter,

You have been one of the best things I have ever done with my life. You helped save me...........

She paused and looked over at Faith who was peacefully sleeping in her crib, it had dawned on her that this was a full circle moment for her. She smiled in the direction of her beloved baby girl and whispered, "Thank you, Mommy! Thank you, God!" and continued her journal entry.

PART TWO

Beautiful

Introduction: Beautiful

The world can be a brutal place for a woman's self-esteem. Everyday women around the world face themselves in the mirror and they assess, "How do I look today? Am I beautiful, pretty, attractive, sexy, or somewhere in between?" It may not be said verbally, but it is an internal dialogue that we have with ourselves. We go out into the world, sometimes, measuring where we fit on the imaginary beauty rector scale based on the number of compliments we might've received or perhaps the number of flirts or stares. The standard placed on being beautiful is so high that even women who by the world's standards reaches it, still harbor some insecurities because now there's pressure to maintain the level of appeal they've become accustomed to.

Destination beautiful is one that starts early and continues well on into our aging years! The truth is real beauty doesn't lay in a woman's physical appearance solely, yet often it's the attribute we judge ourselves most harshly on and so does the world.

In the proceeding pages you will meet Natalie, a woman who has a familiar struggle that many of us face to some degree throughout our lives. Take a peek into her journey as she comes to a crossroads of living within the labels that have been set for her or deciding to find her own way.

Chapter

11

"HE CAN'T REALLY LOVE ME!"

Cramming herself in the wedding dress, she sobbed silently day dreaming of the days when she was a kid, for that was the only time she was 'small'. She had been overweight her whole teen and adult life, now a size 20, her body didn't even recognize itself. She glanced back at an image that she loathed, whispering silently as not to be heard by her best friend and her mother who were waiting outside the dressing room door. "How does he love me? He can't really love me! Look at me, I can't even stand to look at myself."

"What's that you say?" Courtney said hearing her best friend, but not quite able to formulate her words.

Oh uh I was just talking to myself, you know me," she said as she forced out a fake giggle.

"Oh ok, well hurry up, I promised Zack I would make dinner tonight," Courtney responded.

"Okaaayyy, I'm almost done," Natalie said and then quietly sank back into her thoughts. *I won't do it, I can't do it! What was I thinking when I said yes?* She slumped down in the corner, overwhelmed by her thoughts. *He will only cheat on me, or worse, leave me for someone like Courtney who's smaller and more beautiful.* Trying to drown out the thoughts that were pushing her into a fearful place, Natalie threw her head in her hands. Hearing a loud knock on the door startled her back to the present.

"Honey, can we come in? We want to see!" Her mom said.

"Mother! Go away, I need another second!" She exclaimed, irritated.

"But sweetie we've been waiting out here and you've only let us see one dress in the last 30 minutes. Come on, open the door!" Her mother responded forcefully, banging on the door this time.

Natalie breathed deep, then turned around to open the dressing room door. Her mother gasped, "Oh honey, you look absolutely gorgeous!"

Courtney peered over Natalie's mom's shoulder and chimed in, "O-M-G, girl that is THE dress for you! You have got to get it! Jason is going to love you in that one!"

"Honey!" Her mother Cheryl yelled across the room to Natalie's father. Larry peeked over the men's magazine he was reading. He had heard that familiar excited tone in his wife's voice several times in the last hour and a half and usually by the time he made it to the dressing room his daughter would disappointedly say, "NOPE, this is not the dress! I hate the way it fits!" As he rose from his seated position, he fixed his gaze on his Princess coming towards him, he took one look at her and his eyes began to water.

The 25-year-old beautifully curvaceous young lady that he had the pleasure of calling baby girl had morphed into his 5-year-old little Princess all over again. As a child Natalie always wore princess gowns around the house and every evening he knew the moment he got home it wouldn't be Natalie waiting for him it would be Princess Pudding Pop—that's what he used to call her.

She always seemed to know the exact moment he walked through the door. As soon as he entered he would set everything down right at the door and dance Princess Pudding Pop all the way to the dinner table. It was their nightly ritual that lasted well into her 7th grade year when she started to put on more weight and no longer felt like "daddy's *little* girl".

For the first time, he realized he would forever have to share her with another man.

Natalie, noticing a single tear roll down her father's right cheek, walked to him and with the back of her finger wiped it from his face as he had done her so many times.

"What's the matter daddy?" She asked.

"Oh baby girl, you look so beautiful," he said with tears surfacing to his eyes all over again. He grabbed her hand and spun her around just as he had every night when she was five and six and seven on until the age of thirteen. She illuminated with the biggest smile ever and lost herself in the dance with the greatest man she had ever known. They danced as though they were the only two in the room. It was such a sweet fragrance to watch them share such a tender love. They had shared a very close father-daughter relationship, all her friends had envied it—including Courtney. Natalie's mom Cheryl stood close by, she smirked as she interrupted their private dance.

"Honey, soooo what do you think? Isn't this the most beautiful dress?" Cheryl asked as loving as she could. She had spent the last several months attempting to make up for all the years she had abused her only daughter's self-esteem with her obsessive expectations. It was a daily fight to fan the flames of the waging war within her that desired to live vicariously through Natalie.

The **biggest** thorn that had been in Cheryl's side for many years was the envy she felt for her daughter. Their relationship wouldn't have been so strained if it were not for the secret, but not so secret love-hate relationship she had with Natalie.

Natalie had an older brother, Larry Jr. who they called L.J. He was a lot closer to Cheryl when they were growing up. Cheryl decided she didn't want any more children after L.J. and Natalie; she never wanted to bother messing up her almost perfect figure and surprisingly she had maintained it even at 54 years of age.

Before Larry could answer his wife, Natalie said excitedly, "Mother, this is the dress! This is the one!"

"Honey are you sure? It's kind of snug and tight around your stomach," Cheryl countered tugging at the fabric around Natalie's midsection.

Natalie pushed away her mother's nitpicky fingers. *How had she changed her mind so quickly?* Natalie wondered as she looked down at her dress, second guessing herself yet again.

"Well maybe..." Natalie responded, still thinking. Her dad interrupted her by gently grabbing her hand, she turned to face him and their eyes met. Larry didn't say a word, he didn't need to, he just simply gazed into her eyes. With her eyes locked into his, she said with confidence, "Mom this is definitely the one." Larry's eyes smiled, he was proud of her, he knew the fortitude it took for her to stand up to Cheryl—for **anyone** to stand up to Cheryl!

Natalie squeezed his hand tight, her silent gesture of thanksgiving to him for always being her extra dose of encouragement and pushing her beyond anyone's expectations of her—especially her mother's. It was his confidence builders that had encouraged her to be the only girl on her cheer squad in high school that carried 197 pounds on a 5 foot 4 frame. Natalie was beautiful with her reddish-orange naturally curly bouncy locks that she maintained at shoulder length. She was fair skinned with the rosiest red cheeks that hid behind a splash of freckles, characteristics she picked up from her Irish paternal grandmother. She had such an innocent and sweet face. Her shiny green eyes full of wonder always set those closest to her at ease. She wasn't the typical cheerleader, like her best friend Courtney who cheered alongside her in high school, but *became* one nonetheless.

Courtney who was the cheerleading captain was the exact height of Natalie, but was more than 100 pounds smaller. She had curly bouncy locks like Natalie, but was a caramel beauty of mixed origin. Her father was a successful surgeon of Jamaican descent and her mother a professor at Harrison was a Caucasian lady whose roots reached back to Italy.

Natalie walked passed her mom without looking at her. Cheryl turned and looked at Larry with sadness in her eyes. She knew she had done '"it" again. She didn't know what to call "it" or even what it was, but there was always this negative gunk that rose up inside her and she couldn't help, but disapprove of almost everything Natalie did or liked. She had only recently accepted Natalie's fiancé Jason and they had dated for four years.

Chapter

12

MEET THE ROBERTS

Back at work on Monday morning, Natalie tried to keep up with her active second grade class on the playground and to everyone's surprise she was really good at it. There were two things she'd always dreamt of becoming in life, a dance instructor who owned her own studio and teaching elementary aged children. She was so grateful to be doing at least one of the things. In her first year of teaching she had received the best new teacher of the year award. Her dad was always pleased with his over achieving daughter. She loved pleasing her father, but really all her achievements were in an effort to please her mother—to get her to really *see* her. Although, it never seemed to work—not for long anyway. She couldn't remember her mother ever telling her she had done a good job at anything; there was always some form of criticism attached or a sprinkle of 'you could have done a better job at that'. It had gotten to be so detrimental to Natalie's emotional state and her success that she stopped talking to Cheryl about what was going on in her life all together. The only way she knew what was going on with Natalie was to get the information second hand from Larry or her best friend, Courtney.

Natalie and Courtney had been BFFs (Best Friends Forever) since kindergarten. They were like night and day, totally different in appearance and personality, yet inseparable. They had shared everything except for men and underwear, well expect for that one time in middle school when Courtney had a womanly accident in her underwear. It was a bloody mess! Natalie was always overly prepared for everything and had had several extra pair of underwear in her locker, "You never know what could happen," she'd always say. Well *it* happened and Courtney who had always laughed at Natalie's underwear stash was so grateful to her bestest friend in the whole wide world because she had a fresh clean pair of panties to wear.

Courtney knew better than anyone how it pained Natalie to have such a strained relationship with her mother. She tried as much as she could to ease some of their tension and as a part of that "job" she had played the go between, the middle man, for Cheryl and Natalie for years.

Natalie blew her whistle, "Okay boys and girls it's time to line up! Straight line, please," she vocalized very loudly over the rambunctious playground fun. Recess was over and boy was she ever glad, it was so hot outside she felt like she was going to turn into a sunny side egg.

As she guided her class to the water fountain for their water and restroom break, she thought about her Monday night dinner plans with her family. She was nervous, they hadn't seen L.J in almost a year. He had disappeared after having a baby out of wedlock. He was afraid of his mother's disappointment and the drama that would ensue as a result. To keep from having to deal with the conflict, he made the decision to keep his girlfriend and his new baby daughter away to give the family time—well Cheryl time to come to terms with what she called, 'a disgrace to the family name'.

The Roberts where a prominent family in the New Haven, Connecticut area. Larry was the new president of Harrison University, an Ivy League College, and prior to that was the city's mayor. He had carried on the tradition of being a Harrison man like his father who had also been the head of the law department at the university. L.J. had followed his grandfather and father's footsteps and gone to Harrison, but he didn't want anything to do with law or teaching and instead opted for dentistry; which was how Natalie met Jason because he too was a part of the dentistry program at Harrison. Natalie broke the tradition and selected to attend the University of Connecticut. She didn't want to spend her whole life in school and thus became an elementary school teacher.

Then there was Cheryl, the stay at home mom and socialite of the academia world. She had prided herself on raising two almost perfect kids—except for her "fat" daughter and a son who had a child out of wedlock at the age of twenty-eight.

Despite Cheryl's constant nudging and nagging for them to marry, they decided they wanted nothing to do with the institution of marriage. He and his long term girlfriend Lisa of three years loved each other, but both of them weren't sure they wanted to be married. Lisa had come from a divorced family and the marriage ended brutally. And although L.J.'s parents were still married, they were miserable and had been since he was in middle school. It wasn't so much that they had a child out of wedlock that really bothered Cheryl as it was the fact that L.J. wouldn't conform to her standards and that made her furious.

Back at home, Natalie and Jason were frantically rummaging around in the kitchen preparing a simple meal; a family favorite that L.J. loved and had coined it 'Natalie's famous spaghetti'. Natalie and L.J. were very close and it pained her that when he cut Cheryl off, she was one of the casualties of their war.

Jason was cutting up vegetables for the salad and preparing the table. They hadn't moved in together just yet—at least not officially. For the past two years they had spent the night at each other's home every night and were never apart, but to keep up appearances, Jason kept his place and Natalie kept hers. Jason's parents were devout Catholics and they would've been distraught to know that they had been sharing living quarters. Between Natalie's mother and Jason's parents, it was best they kept their living arrangements a secret until they were married and residing in the home they were having built.

No one would've ever put the two of them together, Jason was fit, standing at five foot and eleven inches tall with dark hair, brown eyes, and deep dimples. He was Brad Pitt in the 90's handsome! Natalie was short and portly as her mother called her with a pear shape. She was very unique to look at, yet beautiful nonetheless. Growing up with a very fashion conscious mother worked to her advantage, she had developed her own unique flare for fashion—

conservative, yet trendy. They both knew why their loved worked. When she had no one to understand her, Jason did and when Jason felt all alone Natalie was there. He was never one who let society dictate anything for him and he wasn't going to let what the world thought keep him from a woman with the kindest heart of anyone he had ever known. It was true, he fell in love with her heart first, but that didn't mean he didn't love her physical appearance, he **did**— every single pound.

Dinner was almost ready and Natalie anxiously watched the clock, counting down the time to her family's arrival. Jason had invited his family as a last minute effort to keep the peace. Natalie's mom was one who liked to make everything look perfect so Jason was hoping this would work to their advantage. He endeavored to lessen some of Natalie's concerns about the dinner meeting.

Dinner was schedule to begin sharply at 6:30pm, but the doorbell rang at 6pm on the dot. It was Natalie's parents Cheryl and Larry! Her father brought a bottle of one of his favorite champagnes, Perrier Jouët. Cheryl brought an expensive floral arrangement that she placed in the center of the dinner table—it served as the center piece for the evening. It was an expensive vase Larry bought her as a seventeenth wedding anniversary gift. In the vase included some of Cheryl's most favorite flowers, Hydrangea, Lilly of the Valley, a few Jasmine and several other very beautiful vibrant flowers all gathered together to create a beautiful eye popping symphony. She used to buy Natalie vases with beautiful flowers, but once she got wind that Natalie wasn't using them, she opted to let her 'borrow' some of her most favorite vases and then would take them back home once the evening was complete. Cheryl loved to decorate. It was hard for her not to "push", as her family called it, her ideas and what she thought looked *better* onto her family

Cheryl headed straight for the kitchen after giving hugs to Natalie and Jason. "Natalie, what can I help you with?" She insisted while washing her hands.

Natalie trailing behind her mother, "Nothing Mom, Jason and I have everything taken care of. Please just go sit down in the living room with dad until all the guests arrive," Natalie responded with as much patience as she could muster up.

"Honey, really I don't mind," Cheryl said as she preceded to open up the oven to check on the homemade garlic bread that was still cooking.

"Mother!" Is what Natalie called her when she was frustrated with her. "I'm sure you don't mind," she continued as she chewed her bottom lip. "But, this is a meal Jason and I wanted to prepare for our guests. Please let us finish, we're almost done."

"No, honey I insist," she said as she smiled and grabbed a mixing spoon from the utensil drawer and began to stir the spaghetti sauce.

Natalie, overcome with frustration could no longer hold it in, "Mother, I said...." Jason politely touched her arm, he could hear the elevation in her voice, and he knew if he didn't intervene the next words out of her mouth would not be pleasant.

Cheryl, I think what Nat is trying to say is that tonight is about us serving you, we want to take a load off your busy day, you rest and we'll take care of everything," Jason said.

"Oh Jason, you're so kind. I suppose I do need to rest, as bad as I want to help. Are you sure because I could..." Cheryl paused as Larry entered the room. She was fully prepared for him to insist that she let Natalie and Jason finish the meal without her help. She eyeballed him waiting to hear what he had to say.

"Dear, stop giving the kids a hard time, they want us to rest. Come sit down in the living room with me and watch a little TV until L.J., his family and the Jacobs arrive," Larry said suggestively.

"Okay, okay! But let me make one small insertion to your statement, WE are L.J.'s family, so what family are you speaking of dear?" She said sarcastically.

"Mom, please don't do that. Tonight is going to be a good night. We are going to be respectful and kind to everyone in attendance," Natalie stated.

"Nat whatever do you mean? I'm kind to everyone, but respect, now that must be earned," she said with a smirk to take some of the sting off of her sharp words. Cheryl was very opinionated and passive aggressive. She believed sometimes the truth was brutal, but it had to be. She often masked her callous remarks behind a smile, as though it camouflaged her ill intent.

Shortly after Larry and Cheryl retired to the living room the doorbell rang, Cheryl jumped up quickly anticipating L.J. to be at the door!

Instead it was the Jacobs, Jason's parents, his older sister, her husband and their two children. They had arrived right at 6:25pm, *still* no sign of L.J. Cheryl courteously greeted Jason's family and privately snuck off to Natalie's restroom. She didn't want anyone to see the fear her face held. Their estranged relationship had been one of the worst pains she had ever endured, but she wasn't about to let anyone in on her private anguish. The only person who knew that sensitive side to her was Larry and his loyalty to his wife wouldn't allow him to share that with anyone. That was the main reason he had so much patience with her, he understood her past and what contributed to her being what many referred to as: mean, snobby, or the dreaded **B-WORD**. And although she was all those things to him, at times, he loved her still.

She stood before the mirror with kleenex to her eyes collecting the tears that pooled in the corners before they had time to run down her face dragging mascara and leaving black stains of sorrow all over her face for everyone to see. Holding the pain inside her chest, she felt she could collapse right there on the bathroom floor. A sob tried to break free from her throat, but she swallowed deep to keep it under wraps. *Now is not the time to lose it, keep it together Cheryl,* she said within, coaching herself.

She fixed her golden blonde hair, applied some more lip stick, touched up the foundation underneath her eyes, examined herself one more time to make sure there was no evidence of her mini melt down and headed back to the living room with a smile painted on her face.

Cheryl looked down at her watch, she hadn't realized she had been in the restroom for all of 15 minutes. She saw the clock hanging above the hallway wall, it was 6:45. She scanned the room and the voices still no L.J— her heart sank deeper. She relaxed her shoulders and preceded to the kitchen. Everyone had gathered around Natalie's small island in her kitchen, talking. She stood off observing the laughter and watching Jason's mother interact with Jason, his sister and her kids. She loved their relationship and wished she knew how to duplicate it, but that scenario of harmonious living escaped her. Although she had observed many peaceable interactions, she had no scripts of her own that could emulate such a functional relational way of living; all she knew to produce was a facade of a life she actually loathed. A part of her felt it was too late in the game of her life to go changing things now and she didn't want to bother with the headache of becoming someone different than what she was accustomed to being.

Interrupting the happy energy circulating the room, Cheryl injected, "Whelp, let's eat. I'm sure L.J. isn't coming, no need for us to keep waiting around. Right?!" She asked beguilingly, waiting for someone to agree with her.

Natalie looked at Jason. She had told him on many occasions that she hated that her mother couldn't stand to see people happy and having fun, it was like it made her uncomfortable. Jason desiring to recover the energy that was just vacuumed out by Cheryl's presence blurted out quickly, "Cheryl, let's wait a few more minutes, I'm sure he will be walking through the door any minute."

"Well, if you insist, although this is *still* Nat's house, I'm sure she will agree with you," Cheryl responded and walked out of the kitchen before Natalie or Larry had a chance to address her snide comment. Cheryl went and sat alone in the living room while Larry remained in kitchen with everyone else laughing and enjoying everyone's company. He enjoyed social gatherings, especially with his family. It gave him a chance to breathe and for a moment escape his fast paced and highly stressful life as president of a prominent college and the sterile marriage he lived in with his wife. He liked to golf and so did Jason, they enjoyed talking about the game and the highlights of what was happening in the world of baseball.

Cheryl could hear everyone laughing and it made her cringe within. She strived to look busy on her phone and stay disconnected. She didn't want to feel and she needed to stay as distracted from her feelings as possible so if L.J. didn't show up no one would know that she was crushed. She scrolled through Facebook searching for something interesting to read—with no avail.

Chapter

13

<u>SHE'S BEAUTIFUL</u>

Meanwhile, Natalie was in the kitchen trying her best to relish in all the love and laughter surrounding her, but all she could think about was the clock slowly approaching 7pm and no sign of L.J.—he hadn't even called. She checked her phone for the fifth time, opening it up and searching her text messages, *maybe it chimed and I didn't hear it*, she thought. She pulled up his name only to be disappointed again. The last text from him was two days ago when they had texted about the dinner and her excitement about meeting her new niece who was now six months old. She had only seen pictures of her that Lisa, L.J.'s girlfriend, had sent sporadically.

The clock hit 7pm on the dot and Natalie decided they'd better get dinner started. She had made really creative name placements for each person. She asked Jason to have everyone go sit in the formal eating area so her and Jason could serve them. All the guests sat down at Natalie's long rectangular formal dining table with enough seats for all the adults. Natalie loved to entertain and serve her friends and family, so it was important for her to have a formal dining area in her condominium that accommodated the hostess in her.

They set up a small table adjacent to where the adults were seated with four chairs for Jason's nephews, ages six and four-years-old. As Natalie brought out the salad and set it in the middle of the table, she glanced at the space reserved for L.J. She had placed him right next to her and just as she was about to lose her composure—the doorbell rang. Natalie raced to the door, she knew it was him. She opened the door and leaped into the arms of the man that was standing in front of her. It was L.J. and behind him stood his girlfriend holding their baby girl, Livia.

Natalie couldn't contain her joy! L.J. was just as excited and held his sister in his arms as she cried.

Larry, who was sitting at the head of the table leaned over to his wife and whispered, "Now honey this is a joyous night, please I beg you, be kind." Cheryl relinquished a tiny grin and looked away. Larry rose to greet his son. He had secretly seen L.J. and his family on numerous occasions. It wasn't an easy task to keep their meetings discrete, but he wasn't about to let his wife destroy his relationship with his only son and his new family. However, as to not ruffle any feathers they all pretended as though they hadn't seen each other. He stood behind Natalie beaming with joy as his children reunited—his heart melted. This was a reunion that was long overdue and he was delighted to witness it.

L.J. looked at his father standing behind his sister and wanted to go to him, but Natalie wouldn't let her big brother go, she had missed him deeply. Next to her father, he was the only other man that had been around her whole life who had made her feel secure in the midst of all her insecurities. She felt her dad touch her lower back gently and whisper, "Baby, let them come inside." Natalie was so enraptured in the moment she hadn't paid any attention to the fact that they were still standing in the doorway. Everyone at the table looked on with jollity, except for Cheryl who kept busy on her phone. It was such an emotional, yet beautiful moment, Jason's mom had tears in her eyes and so did his sister. They were all aware of the rift that had taken place in their family, but they had no idea how deep the rupture, but it was clear by Natalie's reaction and Cheryl's distant behavior that it had to be pretty deep and intense.

Natalie finally stepped aside to let everyone in, holding her brother's hand tightly as he reached over to greet his dad with a big hug. Then the baby made a cooing sound and Natalie's attention diverted, "Oh my goodness she's beautiful," Natalie said as she gasped with her hands over her mouth and tears streaming from her eyes. She had well over 50 self-talks over the past week trying really hard to prepare herself mentally for reunifying with her brother and his family, but she could not keep it together. Livia looked so familiar and then it hit her smack dab in the head like a baseball bat—she looked like her when she was a baby! She had the same reddish orange curly hair and green eyes. Natalie couldn't believe it! No one in their family had the same hair and eye color combination as Natalie, except for her and now her niece. Natalie instantly fell in love.

"Oh Lisa, may I?" Natalie asked reaching out her hands to hold Livia for the first time. Natalie and Lisa embraced as they exchanged Livia from Lisa's arms to Natalie's.

Cheryl could no longer resist once she saw her beautiful grandbaby and noticing the resemblance to Natalie—she was captivated. Larry looked back at Cheryl catching a glimpse of love in her eyes, their eyes met briefly then Cheryl bashfully looked back down at her phone. Natalie walked over to Jason carrying her niece and they began to 'ooohh' and 'awww' over her. L.J. grabbed Lisa's hand and escorted her into the room, walking cautiously to the formal dining room where everyone was seated.

They went around the table, greeting and hugging everyone, they started with the Jones family first since they were the closest to the door. Then they walked to the end of the table where Cheryl was seated who appeared to be enthralled in her phone. L.J.'s heart was crumpled, she hadn't even looked up to acknowledge him, but he wasn't about to ruin everyone's night including his own, he leaned over kissed his mother on the forehead and said, "Hello mother. How are you?"

She broke her engagement with her phone, looked up at him with a fake smile plastered on her face and said, "I'm well. Thank you for asking. And you, how are you?"

He looked at his mother longing to really connect with her, he missed her, but he knew she was angry with him and wouldn't allow herself to embrace him. He hated that he had to remove himself from her, but he knew he could never have a chance at a successful relationship with the mother of his child with his mother spewing her negative venom. He respected her and would never speak ill to her so he had to remove himself from her life in order to thrive. L.J. wished that she would accept him and his lifestyle choice, he secretly hoped seeing his daughter would be the thing that would mend their broken relationship.

"We're doing well," he said and he looked back at Lisa who was standing next to him, still holding his hand and now clenching his forearm tightly with her other hand. Lisa was nervous; she longed for Cheryl to receive her and perhaps one day grow to love her. L.J. had shared so many great stories about Cheryl with her, but he had equal shared some very disturbing ones of how she had treated Natalie over the years. She hoped to one day know the Cheryl who was kind and loving. Lisa shared a warm smile with L.J. and then delivered it to Cheryl.

"That's wonderful to hear," she responded. "And how is parenthood?" She directed her question to the both of them.

L.J. looked at Lisa suggestively, trusting she would know that was her cue to respond. She stared at him a moment and then realized what was happening once he squeezed her hand.

"Oh, it's been really good, she's a very demanding baby, but very sweet. She keeps us up late and wakes us up early, but it's been good," Lisa said with a soft giggle trying to relax some of the tension she was feeling.

"And so how is work? Have you gone back?" Cheryl quizzed. That was another issue Cheryl had with Lisa. She was an aspiring artist and Cheryl wanted him to be with someone who had been to college, a teacher would've have even been fine, but not 'some creative, uneducated gypsy' she had called her. She hadn't wanted her to be a stay at home like she had been either.

"Actually, not yet," L.J. injected. "We're thinking she will stay home with Livia for about a year or two, then see where things go from there."

"Humph." Cheryl responded as she cut her eyes.

Larry Sr. who was watching close by thought now would be a good time to join the conversation.

"I think that's a great idea. Your mother staying home with you and your sister was the best decision we ever made. Don't you think so, honey?" He asked Cheryl.

Cheryl paused wanting to give Larry the fish eye, but she didn't want to make a scene and she didn't want to embarrass herself, not realizing that she had already done both. "Yes, it was a really great decision that I don't regret," She said attempting to push back her sarcasm. Only Larry and L.J. detected it.

Natalie and Jason finally joined everyone, Natalie was still holding Livia. She was smitten with her and it was oozing out. "Mom, I have someone you need to meet," Natalie said walking over to Cheryl. The Jacobs at the end of the table watched intently like they were watching a suspense movie, waiting on the edge of their seat to see what would happen next. Everyone seemed to forget that there was yummy food sitting on the table going untouched, except for the kids who were at their table devouring the spaghetti.

Cheryl averted her eyes to Natalie, but immediately Cheryl's attention was snatched away by the beautiful baby in her arms. She tried to deny what she felt, but she knew Livia had already captured her heart. "OH MY look at that hair," Cheryl said as she rose to greet her grandbaby. She gently caressed her hair while looking into her big beautiful green eyes. Almost in a trance-like state Cheryl reached her arms out to hold Livia. Natalie, captivated by the look in her mother's eyes, watched her carefully; it was so unfamiliar, a bit eerie—yet comforting and endearing. She realized there was more to her mother than the mean ole' hag she had known her whole life. She wanted to know the woman behind those gentle eyes.

Natalie gently placed Livia into Cheryl's arms and she held her close. "I can't believe how much she looks like you!" Cheryl said exuberantly to Natalie.

The room was silent, everyone watched attentively. The tense atmosphere that had once polluted the air had been evacuated by the love that had now spilled into the room and was making a lovely mess over everything—including Cheryl's heart.

Livia tugged at her grandmother's dangling pearl earrings, Cheryl was quite the fashionista and enjoyed stylish accessories. Cheryl let out a loud laugh and everyone in the room joined in. For about four solid minutes her attention was fixed on the lovely extension of her legacy, she observed her carefully. Then, abruptly and without warning, she quickly gave Livia back to Natalie. "I'm sorry I need to excuse myself," she said heading for the restroom again.

"Mother, what's the matter?" Natalie asked. But Cheryl just kept walking, pushing past her husband who was standing directly behind Natalie and Jason.

"Let her go baby, she'll be okay. I'm sure she just needs a moment to take everything in; it's an overwhelming day for her," Larry said.

Larry glanced at L.J. who wore a distraught emotional expression smudged all over his face. He was so embarrassed for him, for Lisa— for himself. And, ashamed of Cheryl because she had behaved in very unmannerly ways before, but that night was the worse. Larry knew there was nothing he could say or do to undo what had been done, but at least they could get on with the night and end the nightmare of events as soon as possible. He calmly said, "L.J., Lisa have a seat," as he pulled out Lisa's chair in front of the name placement Natalie had created for her. L.J. sat down next her.

"Thank you Dr. Roberts," Lisa said trying to pretend like the awkward moment that took everyone from harmony to chaos in a matter of minutes didn't just happen.

Larry being the diplomatic, charismatic man that he was, addressed the room attempting to bring the room back to a happy calm. "I think we should eat! I know I'm starved and I'm sure the Jacobs are passed hungry," he said with a smile looking at Mr. and Mrs. Jacobs. They smiled back. "I'll take this lovely lady," he said reaching for Livia. "You and Jason can continue getting everything ready for this ravenous bunch to eat," he said smiling at Natalie. Natalie courteously smiled back and after handing over Livia, she headed for the kitchen with Jason behind her. It was clear that Natalie was disturbed and so was everyone else.

Chapter

14

THE EVIL ONE

Natalie held herself up against the kitchen wall, trying to regain her composure. She had to lighten things up or the evening would be stained by more of her mother's 'ridiculous behavior' as she coined it. She breathed in and out deeply and slowly, while counting in between breaths. It was a technique she had learned in counseling and it really helped her to get centered and regain control. Jason kept an eye her on while he continued to gather everything together for dinner. He had seen her utilize the deep breathing techniques on many occasions and it was always best to leave her alone until she was back to a calmer state.

After about five minutes she joined Jason in the finishing touches. Jason gently grabbed Natalie's shoulders and squared them up with his and he looked her in the eyes checking to make sure she was well. He hugged her tightly then released her. "You have done a great thing here, whatever the outcome, know that your intentions are good and enjoy this space of love you are in now," he said.

She looked at him and smiled. *He's so smart and always knows the right the thing to say at the right time*, she thought. She stood on her tippy toes to give him a kiss and then put on her game face.

They proceeded to the formal dining room. Jason was holding a tray with all the drinks, the bottle of wine his future father-in-law bought, a nice glass pitcher of lemonade and a pitcher of tea for those who didn't want wine, and a another glass pitcher of Evian Natural Spring water. Natalie followed behind him holding a tray of her warm homemade garlic bread.

Lisa stood to help grab the tray from Natalie, but Natalie intervened with, "No, have a seat, tonight we want to serve you."

"Please let L.J. and I help," Lisa replied.

"Okay, if you must," Natalie replied, conceding. She decided to take Jason's advice and allow herself to enjoy the evening, no matter the outcome. She continued, "You and L.J. can grab the pasta and spaghetti sauce. Thank you!"

Cheryl, rejoining the dinner overheard Natalie and cut her eyes sharply at her. She couldn't believe that she would allow them to help after turning down her assistance. Natalie felt a familiar piercing energy beaming at her and she knew exactly where it was coming from. She peeked in the direction of her mother, but Cheryl had thrown her dirty look away before Natalie could see it. She didn't want to offend her mother by turning down her attempts to help with dinner, but she hated her mother's controlling ways. She always found a way to turn 'anything' anyone was doing into a 'Cheryl thing'.

Even though Cheryl was singlehandedly responsible for destroying her dinner and was a constant pain in her rear parts, she loved her mother and wanted to make sure she was okay. She leaned over to her with sincere concern and asked, "Mother, how are you feeling?"

"Oh, I'm fine dear. I thought one of my contacts had fallen out so I went to the restroom to see if it might have fallen onto my clothes. Turns out it had moved to the corner of my eye. Isn't that strange?! I couldn't even feel it!" Cheryl knew that sounded farfetched, but she didn't know what else to say. It was the first thing to escape her lips so she ran with it. She wanted nothing more, in that moment, than for everyone to leave her to her dysfunction.

Natalie looked at her oddly for a few moments. She couldn't believe her mother still had the ability to surprise her—but she did! Cheryl was like a magician's big bag of tricks, you never knew who or what would pop out from moment to moment.

Oh I see what's happening, she is back into character! Well, good, maybe the rest of the night will be less eventful. She thought, while keeping a pleasant look on her face as she responded with, "Good, I'm glad you found your contact."

Natalie eased back into hostess role, pushing what she was really feeling aside. She eagerly wanted everyone to get back to enjoying themselves even though much of the night had been a disaster. She had faint hopes that it could still turn around. She was a pleaser by nature so it was natural for her to conceal her real, raw emotions.

Her therapist had taught her the importance of expressing herself calmly and before her emotions were engaged and heightened. Natalie had two ways of handling conflict, avoidance and angry rage. She wasn't easily incensed, it took her putting up with 'bad behavior' over and over before she welcomed anger's entrance, but when she did anything was subject to fly out of her mouth.

L.J. and Lisa returned to the dining room with the pasta and spaghetti sauce. Everyone sat down—at last dinner was being served. The room finally settled as small talk begin to ensue. L.J and Lisa enjoyed talking with Jason's sister and her husband. Natalie and Jason couldn't get enough of baby Livia, they were preoccupied with her during the whole dinner. Natalie hardly touched her food; it was quite the task to manage an active and curious six-month-old. Jason and Natalie shared some gut-busting laughs each time Livia stuck her hands in Natalie's spaghetti and smeared it all over the table and she even plastered some in Natalie's hair. Livia was a much needed distraction from the chaos—Natalie was enjoying herself indeed!

Jason's parents, the Jacobs, chimed in during certain portions of the conversation with Jason's sister, her husband, L.J. and Lisa. They talked about maintaining a long lasting relationship and the joys of parenting. L.J. and Lisa welcomed the wealth of information from two couples that had been seasoned in marriage and still had lots of live romance and love. The Jacobs had been married for 37 years and Jason's sister who was eight years his senior had been married for 11 years. Larry chimed in with more golf talk with Jason in between his admiration of Natalie and baby Livia.

Cheryl observed the activity in the room, mostly keeping her eyes fixed on Natalie holding her granddaughter and watching L.J. interact with his girlfriend. She could tell that he really loved her and that Lisa shared the same mutual love and respect. They were cute together—even Cheryl couldn't deny that. Deep down she wished she could share the love she felt and express the words she wanted to say, her mind begin to search the guarded places within trying to access the source, but she couldn't properly place her finger on it. What she did knew for sure, however, was that she had to keep everything in her world perfect and she had to maintain that perfection.

Natalie noticed her mother gazing at Livia and thought she'd offer her another opportunity to hold her. She had worked hard at forgiving her mother, but it was a continual process as Cheryl gave her practice, almost daily at forgiving. It had been a little easier since she had been receiving therapy and learning to be sympathetic to the root of her mother's issues. More than anything Natalie wanted a good relationship with her mother, she wanted her to accept her and she wanted her to love her for who she was. No matter how much she hurt her or how angry she made her those feelings never disappeared.

While Larry was talking to Jason he could hear Natalie in the distance say, "Mom!" Immediately his nerves were at attention. He wanted to intervene and he knew whatever Natalie was about to say—it wasn't a good time. Cheryl wasn't the type that could be rushed, she processed things at her own slow pace.

It was too late, the words where already out, "Mom, would you like to hold Livia?" Natalie asked. Everyone quieted their small talk, multi-tasking their attention between their own conversations and Natalie and Cheryl's. No one wanted to look but they didn't want to speak either, the anticipation of Cheryl's answer hung in the room. She wanted to say yes, but it was as if she was always living in a glass house of her own life. She could see what she wanted to show the world, but she couldn't unleash it—it was caged, trapped inside the confined house of self that no one could see, *but her*!

"Oh, you know what I just realized," she said glancing at her Rolex watch, I need to make an important phone call," she smiled politely. "Excuse me," she concluded, leaving the dinner table with her cell phone in hand. That response was all L.J. could stand. He pushed back from the table and rose from his seat, Lisa attempted to grab him, but to no avail, he pulled his arm away.

Natalie looked at him and shook her head no, she knew if he spoke it was going to be the final nail in the coffin that would seal that night as a complete disaster. She mouthed the words, "Please just let her go," to L.J., but he cut his eyes away from her and continued.

The words flung out of his mouth like a torpedo, "Mom, Natalie asked you a question," he said with his heart still aching from his mother's response to his daughter. Faced away from everyone in the room, she wished she had walked out faster, she pivoted to turn around slowly.

"I'm sorry, I don't quite understand what you're saying," she said trying to conjure up the most confusing looking face should could find while trying to make it look sincere.

"Nat asked you if you wanted to hold Livia and you pretended like you didn't hear the question. Mom, Livia is a part of your family, your bloodline, she's your grandbaby, she came from my DNA, your DNA," L.J. pleaded in hopes of convincing her to be level headed. This was his last straw, he was trying to prevent her from creating a calamity that would cause him to go deeper into isolation and this time not returning for even longer, *if at all*. He had already played the scenario out in his head over and over and had even told Lisa that if his mom 'screwed up' this time he was gone and he didn't know when he would let her back into their lives.

L.J. loved his mom, but he had had enough of her controlling and crazy antics. Having Livia made him go into protection mode. He had witnessed her tear Natalie down and diminish her self-esteem and self-love, he was not willing to give his mother the permission to do it again.

For reasons he hadn't figured out she favored him and he always found himself being the mediator between his sister and his mother. He used to try to help Natalie understand their mother's dysfunction until he saw how it affected her, more and more he stepped away from trying to help Natalie understand to becoming angered himself. He could never fathom how a mother could obliterate her only daughter's self-worth. When he made attempts at addressing Cheryl's ill behavior, she pretended like she didn't know what he was talking about. She was good at playing 'the clueless, I haven't done anything' role. While, the scenario might have been new, her behavior was all too familiar to the Roberts family; they had seen it time and time again.

Cheryl's response to Natalie's question overwhelmed L.J with bad memories of his father standing on the sidelines with alcohol and band-aids to medicate and seal up the wounds inflicted by Cheryl. He couldn't let what happened to Natalie happen to Livia. He was going to stand up for his daughter the way he wished his father would've stood up for Natalie. L.J. was one of prevention while his dad was one of intervention and his intervening always came too late—the damage had already been done.

By L.J.'s standards his dad never did enough to protect Natalie from Cheryl's mishandling of her, he was always too diplomatic when he addressed Cheryl about her mistreatment of Natalie. He never demanded that she do anything that brought real change and because of that, whenever the memories surfaced, L.J. became furious with not only Cheryl—but Larry too!

Cheryl wasn't always what she had become. When L.J. and Natalie where younger she was sweet and kind. But, as time went on she changed, and as they grew older she became worse. Her conduct altered the dynamic of their home. Once Natalie stopped greeting Larry at the door in her princess gowns, he started coming home from work later and later. His 'burning the midnight oil' working hours became his alibi for not knowing what was going on in *his* home, however, they all knew Larry stayed busy with work to stay out of Cheryl's way and the havoc she was wreaking at home. He knew she was a tyrant, but even he hated facing her wrath. By default he was an enabler of her destructive behavior.

L.J. looked at his mother with deep intensity, he **needed** her words to be what he wanted to hear. He said a silent prayer in his head, *Lord, please let her say the right thing.* He didn't want to separate from his family again, he loved them, but he wasn't going to allow their dysfunction to bleed into his life with Lisa and Livia. He determined to make a firm stance until his mother changed. He didn't know for sure if she actually would, but he hoped and at the least he wasn't going to enable her!

Cheryl peered back at L.J. and she didn't want to engage him but wanted desperately to get away, it was the only way she knew to keep the peace. Opening her mouth, especially when she was upset was always a bad combination. She hesitated, then the bitter wrath spewed out. "Well, honey to be honest, I haven't heard from you in over a year, then you show up with a six-month-old baby and you don't apologize, you just walk over to me and plant a kiss on my forehead asking me HOW I AM! Do you really care?! Because if you did, you wouldn't have disappeared AND I can't even contact you because YOU changed your number and moved away! YOUR FATHER AND I DON'T EVEN KNOW WHERE YOU LIVE! That's an insult! I've been a great mother to you L.J. and this is how you repay me. You run off with this harlot," she said while slinging her pointer finger in Lisa's direction. Everyone gasped.

Cheryl continued, "Then you have a baby by this trash of a person and you expect me to pretend like nothing ever happened. She took you away from me. The baby has nothing to do with it, you're right she's my family. Sure, I'll hold her," she said walking rapidly towards Natalie who was still holding Livia.

Lisa jumped up from her chair, hurled over to Natalie and grabbed Livia. Cheryl stopped abruptly, "See what I mean, this woman hates me, she's evil!" Cheryl said with anger vibrating in her tone.

Natalie stood up, she joined L.J. in his frustration. She was going to say exactly what was on her mind, there were no hazard signs, no warnings of impeding danger and her braking fluid had just run out, it was all gas fueling her fire and she was HOT, "Mother!! NO, you are the evil one! Why would you say all these vile things to L.J. about the mother of his child?! This is the woman he loves! And you say these despicable things right in her presence, in front of a room full of people. What is wrong with you?!" Natalie asked as her voice began to shake with emotion.

It had been a few years since Natalie had allowed her mother to bring her to the point of stooping to her level with mean words and hurling insults, but she had had enough! Her dinner party was already ruined and she felt horrible that Cheryl had spoken to Lisa the way she had. She felt a strong obligation to defend her.

L.J. came up behind Natalie and gently touched her shoulder as he had done many times when they were younger, that was his attempt at calming her and reassuring her that she wasn't alone and she could allow him to take over. Still enraged, Natalie scrambled for her seat. She was trembling, an affect that was a result of her fury. Natalie tried to avoid conflict at all cost because of the aftermath that lingered within her as a result—but it was well past too late! The words were out and the atmosphere was sick with hateful words causing her to feel even sicker.

As though it was some type of brother/sister tag team duo, L.J., picked up where Natalie left off. "I'll tell you what's wrong with her. She's insecure, mean, hateful, and unhappy and she hides it under this fake exterior of, 'Oh my life is perfect! We are the Roberts, we have it all together! Why, yes dear my marriage is perfect! Why, yes of course I'm happy!' He said mocking her. "While you sit back and shred everyone around you apart bit by bit, killing them from the outside in! I wonder how long dad will last!" He exclaimed. Cheryl clutched her pearls.

Larry stood up, "That's enough! I will not sit here and watch you talk to your mother in such a disrespectful manner!" Larry gaining control over his emotions, cleared his throat and exchanged his loud booming tone, for a more calm and concerned one, he continued, "L.J. this is so unlike you. Please, son have a seat, calm yourself. We can have a discussion without all the anger"

"Dad, you're right I was out of line." He glanced at his mother briefly and said, "Mom, I'm sorry."

He had never spoken to his mother like that, but she had never hurt him so deeply. It was years of confined frustration that had spilled over and out of his mouth. Even when he went into protective mode for Natalie he knew how to keep the fine line of being direct and assertive without being disrespectful. All those years he had kept his real feelings bolted up and locked away. He was so embarrassed, his behavior was out of his character.

He let his eyes search everyone in the room as he offered up a sincere apology, "I'm really sorry for my behavior tonight everyone. I allowed my emotions to overtake me." He turned to Natalie, "I'm sorry I ruined this special evening you and Jason planned for us," then he followed his words with a warm hug.

He looked to Larry again, "Dad I'm sorry for speaking to your wife in such a disrespectful manner, please forgive me."

Although his mom deserved a good cursing, he felt remorseful. She wasn't the worse person in the world, just close to it, but even so he was a reverential man and no mother ever deserved to be spoken to so harshly by their child. He addressed his mother once more, "Mom,

I'm sincerely sorry." Tears begin to well up in Cheryl's eyes, she looked away so that L.J. wouldn't see them.

"Natalie and Jason, thanks for a, an, a...," he searched hard for a kind, yet honest word to describe the evening, but couldn't find one, "a night, thanks for a night." Lisa and I are going to get out of here. I hope you all enjoy the rest of your evening." He said as he motioned for Lisa, who was still in disbelief over what had just taken place.

"Brother, please stay!" Natalie pleaded, hoping to convince him to stay a while longer.

"Really, it's ok. Its best I leave, but don't worry we will be in touch soon. I love you!" He said grabbing her hand and holding it enduringly. He distributed a cordial smile to everyone before he and Lisa with Livia in her arms headed for the front door.

Natalie clasped her head in her hands, she was disappointed and couldn't conceal it, but she wasn't the only one, everyone knew how she felt—*because they felt it too*. They all wished the night had gone better, even Cheryl.

Chapter

15

<u>HER CLOSEST COMPANION</u>

Natalie woke up in the middle of the night and her heart still ached, the only remedy she knew that would numb the pain was her familiar comfort—FOOD! It made her happy; it took her mind off her issues and wrapped her up in yummy, juicy, deliciousness! Food made everything better! She was a perfectionist and when things went awry—she ate, when things went bad with her family—she ate, when her mom had a crazy episode—she ate. However, it wasn't only tragic things that caused her to yearn for food, happy moments equally called for food because well, what better way to celebrate than to eat a delectable meal!

That night she ate and ate and ate until she couldn't eat anymore. She started off with a whole bag of chips, dip, and a big bowl of chocolate ice cream in the kitchen. Then moved to her bedroom with some left over spaghetti and to wash it down a bottle of her favorite drink, crème soda. She popped in one of her favorite movies,

Sleepless in Seattle. *What would be better than watching one of my classic favorite movies in bed accompanied with some of my amazing spaghetti?* Just the thought of it made all the lamenting she had been doing over the night's events disappear.

Throughout her life food had become her closest companion. It evacuated all the pain, rescued her from loneliness, and buried the rage that snowballed inside her as a result of being made fun of in school and the constant rejection she faced from her mother.

The torture all started for her on her first day of middle school. She wore her favorite dress in her favorite color. It was a sunflower yellow that fit loose and went past her knees. In an attempt to be trendy like her mother, she topped it off with a blue jean jacket, the perfect pair of matching flat ankle boots that were blue jean material with a yellow flower in the stitching, and peaking just above her boots were a pair of turquois boot socks that she scrunched up. She wore a cute turquois necklace and earring set. She had learned the art of embracing colors from her mother and had intended on being the most fashionable 7th grader at school. Although she knew her body type was different from her friends they all had accepted and embraced her and her dad always made her feel special and beautiful. Cheryl helped her with her desired look by gathering her long luscious red hair and braided into one side braid that hung over her left shoulder.

She topped her look of with a hint of a very faint pink lip gloss that made her already very pink rosy lips glisten and shine. The night before she snuck some of her mother's Lancome mascara, but she wouldn't miss it because her make-up drawer was full of numerous types of mascara, lipstick, and eyeliner; she had so much make-up it was almost like a cosmetic store and it was just as organized too. She applied just a little mascara enough to accent her green eyes, but not too much. She was a 'good girl' and she didn't want her mother thinking of her as a mascara thief, especially since Cheryl had forbidden her to wear mascara until at least the 9th grade, but that felt like eons away to Natalie. She felt it was unfair, but she would never tell her mother that she would just sneak some mascara and not look into her eyes until after school, but by that time she would have smudged it off.

Natalie stepped out of her mother's Volvo mini SUV, she looked pretty and she felt it too! She had planned what she was going to wear several weeks ago and had even tried it on numerous times. Each time her dad told her she was going to be the most beautiful girl in school, while L.J., who was entering his sophomore year in high school, threatened to come to her school and blacken any boy's eye who talked to her. Of course Cheryl added her negative commentary about the dress looking a little too snug and adding, "maybe you should consider wearing a black dress that will help you look much smaller." Natalie knew enough of her mother to know that was her nature she had to always find something wrong with her, so she opted to believe what her father and brother said of her instead. *I look beautiful!* she thought, smoothing her hair into place as she proceeded into the school looking for Courtney and a few of her other friends.

As Natalie walked into the school she noticed a lot of people starring and whispering, some even pointed and snickered. At first she thought they were commenting on how beautiful she looked until she heard one boy she had gone to school with since elementary sing out, "NASTY NATALIE SITTING IN A TREE LOOKING FOR SOMEONE TO

KISS, BUT SHE'S TOO FAT AND UUUGGLLYY!!" He laughed as a chorus of laughter joined him from all the other students who surrounded her in the hall. She had finally spotted Courtney and the other girls within the crowd of mockers, everyone was laughing, except for Courtney—a faithful, loyal friend who would be her only friend throughout middle school.

She had started to pick up weight in the 6th grade and over the summer she had put on more pounds and was bigger than most the girls in 7th grade. From that day on Natalie would never be the same. That night when Larry came home from work, he stood at the door waiting for his Princess Pudding Pop to greet him, but she never came; instead he found a crying *teenager* buried in her room and wanting to be left alone.

On many days Natalie came home crying because of the evil jokes at school. She hid her pain from Cheryl because she wasn't capable of comforting her or even understanding. She could only imagine her advice being along the lines of things she had already said to her like, "Oh honey you need to lose weight, you're a pretty girl, but most can't see it because you're hiding yourself in layers of fat." Since Larry came home so late on most nights she didn't trouble herself with talking to him about it much either. He was good at boasting her self-esteem though, so in moments when she felt like a "hideous beast" she could always count on her daddy to restore her confidence.

The only other person who knew the full weight of what she was carrying other than Courtney was L.J., and he was the over-protective big brother who had defended her so many times and made the tainting stop. L.J. was so popular and well known that his popularity still lingered at his old middle school where Natalie attended. Once

Natalie finally broke down and told him what was going on at her school, like any great brother he came to her rescue, even against Natalie's wishes. She loved how he loved her, but she didn't need anyone to stand up for her. It was a good thing he stepped in because by the beginning of the next school year, much of name calling had ceased. But, L.J. couldn't make people be nice to her and since she knew if she told him she was still dealing with cruelty, he would be driving up to her school throwing around his clout and threatening the boys who were treating her maliciously—she kept it to herself. And she suffered in silence with her companion—food, it always remained close and made everything better.

At times her mind still played the malevolent song that had become her 7th grade school anthem. Food was her outlet and whenever she was made fun of it welcomed her, no rejection, no mean words, no judgment, just comfort, acceptance and peace.

Natalie set up in her bed resting her back against her pillows, eating spaghetti and watching the movie. Just as in times past she waited for comfort to fill the place occupied by chaos, but there was still a gnawing, she paused the movie half way through to take the empty spaghetti bowl back to the kitchen. While in the kitchen it dawned on her that she and Jason had made a lot of garlic bread and there were still leftovers. Natalie went to the fridge to get one to heat up in the microwave, but one didn't satisfy the gnawing that was still eating away at her subsequently one turned into three.

I can't believe I just ate all that, she thought. She was beyond stuffed, the gnawing had dissipated, but now she was left with regret and a really sick feeling in her stomach. She vowed that she wouldn't eat anymore that night and would even skip breakfast and lunch, but first she had to relieve the pressure on her stomach, it ached badly.

Natalie darted to the toilet, got on her knees, with her face over the toilet seat, she shoved her fingers deep into her throat until the food she had just ate emerged and dribbled out of her mouth and was swimming inside the toilet. After she forced everything out that would come forth she laid down on her back, tired, her eyes still watery and her throat seething with the feel of acid sitting on it. Her mouth felt filthy and it smelled of wet sewer, but she finally felt better. She fell asleep right there on her bathroom floor.

Chapter

16

<u>QUEEN LATIFAH</u>

Natalie woke up the next morning and was greeted with a slap in the face, the concerns about the night before still loitered in her head. She had punished her body to feel better and still woke up feeling worse. She stumbled to her bedroom to turn off the alarm clock that was still ringing loudly. She had so many thoughts swirling in her head, creating a mixed up mess. Natalie loathed how the whole evening went, she hated that her mother was so evil, she felt awful for Lisa and L.J., she was angry at herself for responding so harshly to her mom, she longed to have peace in her family, perhaps the kind they had never known, and she felt deep remorse for the episode she had with food and the toilet. It had been one of her worst days in long time, she hadn't had a blow up with her mom in a while and it had been eight months since she had binged and purged.

She had been doing so well the past few weeks on her regiment of exercising, eating healthier, and portion control that she had dropped more than 10 pounds. Natalie hoped to be in a least a size 16 by her wedding, she really wanted to be in a size 12, but she knew neither goal was realistic, considering she only had three months to get there, she wasn't even sure if a year would be enough time. The last time she wore a size 16 she was around 15 years old and she couldn't even remember ever being a size 12.

Natalie was doing everything she knew to lose weight, she was even aware of her food triggers. She had been on enough weight loss exhibitions and had tried every weight loss program out, she knew what to do and what not to do and her trainer had taught her the importance of journaling her meals. The journey of losing weight was something like a full-time job and even when she wasn't doing anything associated with weight loss or eating, losing weight was always on the forefront of her mind. It consumed her. She knew she wanted to lose the weight, but could she really do it, she had been unsuccessful so many times she often questioned herself.

She was determined to hold fast to the promise she made to herself that she wasn't going to eat breakfast, but she was starving and her stomach kept reminding her of that fact as it growled at her. One thing her therapist taught her was to keep the vision of where she wanted to be before her, along with a confession that she could recite every morning and every evening. She kept those images on her bathroom mirror so that she was reminded to say them and see the pictures day and night. Sometimes she visited the picture and confession several times throughout the day. She had taken a picture of both items and would refer to them on her phone. Whenever she was in a bad place emotionally she clung to those artifacts. Natalie wished she would've remembered to run to her restroom before she ran to her kitchen. But, the thick chaos from the evening clouded her judgment and all she could see was comfort and peace and that equaled food!

She returned to the restroom and begin to recite her confession while looking at the picture and every now and again she scanned herself until she could see herself the size of the woman in the picture. Natalie wasn't quite sure how much she weighed but she was a full sized lady who carried her weight in a way that she wanted to, boldly and with confidence. In her mind that lady was a size 12. The picture that she kept on her mirror was of Queen Latifah, she was a tall black woman with very large breasts and while Natalie's frame was no comparison, what she loved most about her was her confidence. She only wished she possessed a fraction of it. It wasn't about a body image as much as it was about what she exuded. *You have to be someone pretty secure to add Queen in front of your name*—Natalie love it.

Sure, it would've been ideal to place a much smaller woman on her mirror, someone like a Jennifer Aniston, Carrie Underwood, or perhaps even Drew Barrymore all who were about her height, but Natalie was a realist. She had never been that tiny and couldn't foresee ever getting there and since she knew one of the first steps to reaching your goal is to first see it, she didn't dare put their images on her mirror. Besides there was something about the way full-sized black women carried their weight that Natalie was in love with!

Several months ago, Jason and Natalie had visited some friends in the Hollywood area. The guys had planned some guy time while the ladies took Natalie to a talk show—The Queen Latifah Show! Natalie was instantly fascinated by her, she loved her stride, the way she held her head when she walked in a room—she owned it! From then on

Natalie was a fan! She spent the next few weeks following her visit to the show watching all things Queen Latifah, all her old movies and even a TV show called, Living Single. Her favorite movie though was, Set It Off! Jason laughed at her obsession on many occasions, but he did enjoy watching Living Single with her, it became their nightly thing when he stayed at her house.

Natalie read the list of motivational words attached to her mirror that were written in big bold letters.

"I am beautiful!

I am smart!

I am love!

I am loving!

I accept me for who I am!

I love me!

I..."

Just then she heard a loud ringing sound that abruptly put a halt to her confessions. It was her home phone. She was confused. *Who would be calling me so early in the morning and on my home phone*? She wondered, Natalie hurried to her bedroom phone that was sitting on her nightstand. Noticing her parent's home number on the caller ID she hoped it wasn't bad news.

"Hello!" She said frantically and out of breath.

"Well, hello to you dear! And just why are you out of breath? Are you working out?! I sure hope so."

She recognized the voice on the other end of the phone. "Hello, mother! Yes, as a matter of fact I *WAS* working out. I was just in the exercise room lifting 300 pounds on the weight machine you bought for me!" She responded sarcastically.

That was the sum of how their 'fall outs' went, Cheryl would do or say something that pushed Natalie to the edge, Natalie would 'lose it', say some harsh things to her, become sick with regret for how she spoke to her mother, then binge and purge. Cheryl on the other hand would go on as if nothing ever happened.

Prior to this cycle Natalie never stood up for herself, she would wait for Jason to intervene or vent to her dad. But, after around her second year in college she was *done* being degraded by her mother. However, it took her mother *standing on her nerves* several times before the lid blew, but when it blew it blew all the way off. During her college years Natalie lashed out a lot, mostly at her mother, but she didn't like who she had become. She was defensive and angry all the time and even with all fiery passion that she constantly spewed at her mother—it never changed her. Cheryl could have a huge yelling match one night and the next day you would think it never happened. She just went on, no apology, no explanation, she just continued on.

"Oh honey, must you be rude to your mother?"

"Sorry, mom I wasn't trying to be rude," she said gritting her teeth. She continued, "It's early, I'm getting ready for my children. How may help you?" She asked in the politest way that she could.

"Well, I just uh, I just..." She searched for the right way to ask. But, before she could dress it up and put a pretty bow on it, it came out hurried and not as polished as she had hoped. "I am just curious about what you thought of last night? Was I really that mean? I'm just hurt and rightfully, so don't you think?"

Leave it up to mom to make sure all the questions have a slant in her favor, Natalie thought. "I can't get your dad to see my point of view, I thought maybe you'd understand since we're both ladies and all."

"Well mom, I really don't think it's my place to get involved. I do think that it would be kind of you to apologize to L.J. and Lisa."

"Now why on planet earth would I ever do that?"

"Well I don't know mom, maybe because you insulted them and they are hurt." She said struggling to evict all emotion from her voice so Cheryl couldn't detect her frustration with last night and her anger with her for always being a *female dog*. True indeed, Natalie had picked up some of her mother's ways, she never uttered a curse word not even in her head because her mother trained her that ladies never used swear words. Although Cheryl never needed to curse to insult you and make you feel like hot poo from a sick dog's butt, all she had to do was use her arsenal of wicked words and totally annihilate anyone with the vile venom that spewed from her tongue.

"Dare we discuss hurt? And what of mine? I have my share. You ARE aware of that, right?"

Natalie really wanted to say, *Oh really, YOU know how to hurt, I never deemed that possible*, but instead she said, "Mom, can we continue this conversation later. I really must go or I'm going to be late for work."

"Oh yes I'm sorry." Cheryl was really self-absorbed and she was hardly ever respectful of other people's time because she had so much leisure time. She kept talking, "But wasn't that a gorgeous baby?" Getting lost in her own fairytale thinking she continued, "I would LOVE to be a part of her life, to baby sit her and even have her stay several nights with me. Oh that would be so much fun!"

Natalie thought, *stay SEVERAL NIGHTS, it would be a cold day in hell before L.J. and Lisa would allow her to even stay ONE day with you!*

Natalie stirred the conversation back to her original intent, "I hope you will consider making amends with all parties involved and fix things so that scenario can become a possibility in the future," Natalie responded.

Cheryl gasped, "You don't think it is possible now? Maybe, if you intercede for me, you know just talk to your brother on my behalf...tell him I didn't mean to say what I said..."

Ah ha and there it is, that's what she really called for and with that Natalie's thoughts carried her attention away from her mother's manipulating words.

Natalie interrupted her before she could finish, "Mother, really I must go."

"Oh, those little stinkers can wait."

"MOTHER!" Natalie said outraged.

"What?! I have told you many times you are wasting your gift teaching those little rascals. You should be teaching at a university somewhere, it doesn't have to be Harrison! You're so smart Nat and you waste it on those, those, those gremlins! Go back to school Nat, get a master's and a doctorate degree and teach at a university," Cheryl insisted.

Natalie counted slowly to ten in her head while her mother spoke, drowning out her words. She couldn't bear another offensive word especially about her 'children', whom she loved dearly.

"Mom I don't mean to be rude so forgive me if I am, but I'm going to hang up the phone now. I MUST get ready for work. Thank you for calling and have a good day!" Then Natalie gently hung up the phone, she didn't even give Cheryl a chance to say good-bye. She breathed a sigh of relief, Natalie was proud of herself, she wouldn't have been able to handle her so well in the past. She had learned in counseling to, *"never give your power away by losing control, even if you feel provoked because once you give your power away you render yourself powerless!"* She could hear her therapist's voice ringing in her head, she would've made her so proud.

Cheryl sadly hung up the phone. She wished she knew how to be better, she had tried counseling several times over the past few years, but it never seemed to work. She hated counseling, it made her dig up too many uncomfortable feelings and she didn't like being uncomfortable. Any time she felt emotions arise that made her feel uncomfortable she would immediately push them back.

Being true to 'Cheryl fashion' she allowed sadness to invade her space for about two minutes after she hung up the phone, then she pushed that feeling aside, smooth her hair back into place, sprung up from her seated position and said, "Whelp I guess I better prepare for my ladies' tea gathering today." Once a week she held a tea gathering for the ladies who like her where married to professors at Harrison, a few ladies from her church, several of the women in her neighborhood and a few friends. They were some of the who's who socialites in town, many who were spouses that stayed home, but dedicated time to head up successful charities and do some great and positive things in their communities. The ladies met about various issues, some important matters, other times just gossip and many times a good mixture of the two.

Chapter

17

<u>THE CHERYL EFFECT</u>

Walking by her pantry she dug in the far back and pulled out a box of half eaten Krispy Kreme donuts. She opened it up and inside were four Krispy Kreme glazed donuts, she smiled and made haste to pour herself a cup of freshly brewed coffee. *I will only eat one, okay two, but that's it,* her voice echoed in her head. Her heart began to pump fast with anticipation as she sat down in front of the donuts and coffee. She dipped the donut in the coffee as steam swirled around the top. Natalie leaned over and lifted it to her mouth, it was warm sweet ecstasy dripping down her throat, a feeling that nothing could compare to.

As she took another bite she replayed the conversation that she just had with Cheryl in her head and substituting what she said with what she wished she would've said. *Mother, just shut up! No, that would've been way too harsh. Stop playing the victim! Nah, that wouldn't have went over to well. Why must you be so selfish?! Yeah, that wouldn't have worked either. Hmmmm....* She breathed deeply as her thoughts concluded, she looked down at the empty box before her and sulked. Those donuts were such a pleasurable comfort, she hadn't realized that she had eaten all four. They didn't try to control her, they didn't insult her, they had no expectations of her, they didn't get on her nerves, they just made her feel calmer, happier, better. That same high wave she was riding on sent her crash landing back to the dark abase of her negative emotions with no parachute.

Immediately she was hit with guilt as she sat in front of the empty box. "Oh my God! I ate all FOUR! Why do I let her affect me like this?" She sulked all the more! It was the *"Cheryl affect!"*

Finally pulling herself together, she rushed out the door. She would have to speed to make it on time. As she pulled into the parking spot that read, "Teacher of the Year" she heard a reminder chime from cell phone.

It was a text message from her brother: I'M SORRY AGAIN ABOUT LAST NIGHT. I HOPE THIS DIDN'T AFFECT YOU NEGATIVELY. IF YOU WANT, I'D LIKE TO INVITE YOU TO MEET ME AT THE GYM LATER, IT'S BEEN AWHILE SINCE WE'VE WORKED OUT TOGETHER.

Natalie responded with a quick: HELLO BROTHER! IT'S GREAT TO HEAR FROM YOU! I'D ABSOLUTELY LOVE TO MEET UP WITH YOU FOR A WORKOUT. LET'S MEET UP AT 5PM! She hit send then moved quickly to the school building. She only had five minutes before the kids could start making their way to her classroom.

Natalie was very well organized—she over planned for *everything*. She was such a thorough planner she even had several pair of gym clothes in her car in the event that she ever wanted to work out right after work. Sometimes she would go walking at a local walking and trail park not too far from her work. It was a great way to alleviate stress, think, and burn some calories. She tried at all times to be prepared for the unexpected. It was her strategic planning along with her cutting edge teaching style and the fact that she cared deeply about each child who walked through her classroom that secured her the coveted special parking space and "Teacher of the Year" for the last three years that she had been a teacher.

John F. Kennedy Elementary School was her first teaching job right out of college and it was her first choice. Her mother always called her an overachieving under achiever because she believed she always overachieved at whatever she did, but that she always set the bar too low for herself. Cheryl always wanted her to be a professor and she was smart enough to be, but she could never figure out why Natalie didn't pursue it.

Her father on the other hand was overjoyed at the work she was doing. He loved her courage to be bold and do what she really loved, despite what anyone else wanted her to do. He just wanted her to be happy and it pleased him that she was.

Breathing heavily, she made it to her classroom and flopped in her chair. She rested her head in her hands, attempting to calm herself. Even though her 'special parking' space was closer to the school building it was still a very extensive walk. Catching her breath, she took a sip from her bottled water. She figured since she had made such poor eating choices the night before and that morning she'd better try to redeem herself and have a balanced lunch because working out with her brother was always serious business.

L.J. never went easy on her, he pushed her to the max and that was the sum of their relationship. He always challenged her to her highest best and even pushed her beyond what she believed she could do. However, when she fell short he never condemned her and that was one of many reasons he was her very best friend most of her life and up until his recent disappearance they had talked every day.

Natalie finally admitted to herself that she was a bit bitter, but was able to balance her toxic emotion with logic. Even though she didn't know all L.J.'s reasons for disappearing from her life, she trusted him enough to believe that if he did something that drastic then there had to be a very good reason. Despite her feelings in the matter she was very excited that they were going to hang out and she could hardly contain her joy!

She couldn't wait for the day to speed by, which was rare because she loved being with her "children". The only other day she was ready for the day to hustle along was on Friday, which was her and Jason's date night. Although they had dated every week, sometimes twice a week, for the last four years, it always felt new and fresh. Dating Jason never got old or boring for her, she loved that man!

Natalie missed Jason's company last night. He had forgotten to feed his dog before he left to Natalie's for dinner and immediately raced home after all the guests left to do so. He lived 35 minutes from her so he decided to stay home once he got there. They hardly stayed a night apart, but it was late and they were both tired. She was partially glad he hadn't stayed the night with her. She had kept only one secret from him all the years they had been together and that was her binging and purging episodes. It wasn't a secret she tried to keep on purpose, she just simply never felt the need to binge and purge when he was around. Most days his presence alone made all her insecurities, her fears, and her heartache disappear—he was simply good for her. Since she had never binged and purged in his presence she didn't see the need to discuss with him something he had never witnessed. It just seemed irrelevant to her.

Her fast paced breathing had waned and heart was no longer pounding—she was relaxed. Sitting quietly at her desk the first thought that flooded her mind was Jason. She sent him a quick text before her first student of the day came through the door. It read: **M.Y.L.C.!** It was an acronym that meant 'Missing You Like Crazy!' Because Jason was a busy dentist, he hardly ever had time to text while he was at work and Natalie took her job very seriously so when she was with her "children" she never looked at her phone. Consequently, they developed quick acronyms that they could send to each other whenever they had a free moment.

Before Natalie knew it, it was 2:45pm and the kids were finishing up their last assignment for the day. The bell rang promptly at 3pm signaling an end to the school day. Natalie lined the class up to walk them to the gym where they then split into their respective areas to be transported home. She walked swiftly back to her classroom, she was filled with exhilaration!

Chapter

18

<u>BABY SISTER</u>

Natalie settled in her car, it was a long 40 minute drive to her brother's favorite gym in the city. It was across town and was even a ways away from where Natalie lived, but L.J. was worth every minute and more.

She had changed her clothes before leaving for the gym, she hated changing in the gym dressing room with all the little petite girls, she often wondered why they came to the gym in the first place with their flat tummies, little bean pole arms and legs and perky breasts. She loathed dressing in front of them, it reminded her of her cheerleading days and being the only 'big girl'.

Arriving at the gym with 10 minutes to spare she waited patiently in the car for L.J. to arrive. She wasn't a member of the gym, but she could accompany L.J. as a guest on his 'buddy pass'. As Natalie waited she listened to her favorite country singer Carrie Underwood belt out tunes from her song, "Look at me". She picked up her phone to re-read Jason's responses again. She loved reading his sweet texts over and over again. She knew he had to have really missed her too, because he hadn't used acronyms instead he typed full sentences. It read: "Oh Sweetie, I'm missing you so much more! I can't wait to see you tonight! I have thought about you every Minute of the day today Mrs. Jacobs! My thoughts were so vivid of you I could smell you! I love you with every breath I breathe! Okay honey, gotta run!" She chuckled at his last sentence, that was so Jason to pull her in with his sweet honey then jump back to being focused on his work, but it didn't bother her, it was amusing. Her father was the same way. Besides, her eyes kept gravitating to "Mrs. Jacobs" and she loved when he called her that, although it wasn't official, the clock was ticking quickly to the day that it would be.

Mrs. Jacobs!!! I just LOVE the sound of that! I'm at the Gym waiting for L.J., he invited me to workout with him today! I'm really looking forward to it! I can't wait to tell you all about it and my conversation with mom this morning! I.L.Y.2.I. M.OM.S.!" she texted. I.L.Y.2.I M.O.M.S. was another "one of their frequently used acronyms that stood for, I love you to infinite mate of my soul (soulmates). As she hit send on her cell phone she heard a loud bang at her window, she looked over and saw a face pressed against the glass. She jumped so violently that her arm flung and hit the stirring wheel sounding the horn loudly throughout the parking lot! It was her brother, L.J.! He was quite the prankster and had been since they were young children. He always loved getting a scare out of her.

"Oh my God L.J. are you crazy?!" She yelled through the window, hyperventilating, her heart still pounding through her chest! L.J. laughed.

Natalie gathered her workout bag that housed her sweat towel, water bottle and ponytail holder. She was still shaken as she fidgeted while getting out of the car. L.J. feeling a little remorse for his scare gone wrong, grabbed her workout bag from hands, making it easier for her to get out the car. When she got out of the car she slapped his arm, "L.J. don't do that again, geez!" They both laughed! Following her sibling love tap, she reached out her arms to hug him and they embraced. L.J. had his arms wrapped around her back and immediately Natalie became self-conscious. She hated when people "felt it", "the fat". Even though she knew L.J. loved her just the way she was and didn't judge her, she couldn't help but be consistently aware of her body. She always held her weight in her mind and wondered what people were thinking about her. Sometimes she didn't have to wonder, there had been times when she would be out eating or shopping for clothes and she could hear people whispering about her or staring, especially when she and Jason were together. She was fully aware that people wondered what he saw in her.

She had heard her whole life that she had a beautiful face and she hated that. She wanted to be told her whole person was beautiful not just an isolated portion of her, it was like she was divided into segments, and only 25% of her was acceptable and appealing. When she was younger she would pretend that it wasn't a part of her, like it was just something that followed her around, like an evil twin that wouldn't go away. Her face was the likeable twin and her body was the evil twin and whenever she wanted to feel more confident she would simply disassociate herself with the evil twin, like it didn't exist and that was how she was able to be such a confident cheerleader.

L.J., unaware of his sister's thoughts, held her closely, he had missed his best friend. He loved her just the way she was, but as a health fanatic his only concern had always been her health and her self-esteem. L.J. was fit and had been since his days of playing baseball in high school. After he graduated from high school he coupled his fitness lifestyle with eating healthy. He and Lisa had both explored being vegan for a few years, but decided to introduce meat back into their diet when Lisa had gotten pregnant with Livia.

Unlike Natalie who was short L.J. stood eye to eye with their dad standing at exactly six-feet tall and was quite the looker. He had also inherited his dad's dark black hair. He was lean and chiseled. He had always been into fitness and despite his ultra-preppy appearance he was a really down to earth caring kind of guy. A dentist like Jason he had the most beautiful white, straight and sparkling teeth. You could almost hear a sound effect whenever he smiled, 'ding'! When he looked at you with his deep piercing brown eyes, it always seemed like he knew something you didn't. He was very wise for his age and extremely protective of his family, especially his little sister. This made it all the more difficult for him to step away from her when he cut his mom off, but it was the only way he knew to protect her from the backlash Cheryl was sure to bring down on her if he remained close to Natalie. She would've punished Natalie for it and made her feel bad about their closeness, she was extremely manipulative. Since L.J. had made up in his mind that he wasn't going to have anything to do with Cheryl for any reason he wouldn't be able to go into protective brother mode for Natalie when Cheryl did harass her about him. Consequently, it just made more sense to him to excuse himself from her life as well. Natalie wasn't his target, but she was a victim of their family dysfunction!

After giving his sister one of his signature tight hugs, he stood back holding her shoulders and looking her over. He needed to know that she was okay in his absence, he had felt a tremendous amount of guilt about this decision. Natalie looked at him sheepishly, smiled, and then looked away quickly. He knew what that look meant, but it was too early to start asking questions, he needed to give her time to warm up to him again and a good workout would do the trick. It wasn't by chance that he asked her to come workout with him, they needed just the right amount of quality time mixed in with the distraction of working out and what he called fluff talk, then the real heart to heart stuff could occur naturally.

"So baby sister, how are you?" L.J. asked as he opened the door for Natalie and they entered the gym. He had frequented the gym often, so he didn't stop at the counter to show his pass, he just gave a polite wave, smiled and kept walking.

"I'm pretty good!" She responded, trying to sound excited. She didn't want the day to be about her, but about him, how he had been adjusting to his new family and if he was going to be permanent fixture in her life again. She desperately wanted to conceal her anger at him for being absent during some of the most amazing moments in her life. She couldn't handle him vanishing again and she couldn't wait for the right moment to tell him so—in a very polite manner of course. She enjoyed having harmony in her relationships which made it easy for her to tuck away any uncomfortable emotions she felt and "eat her voice away" as her therapist termed Natalie's way of handling stress and conflict. She loathed being at odds!

He looked at her again this time checking to see if there was some residue in her eyes of how she was really doing, but she avoided his gaze. "That's good to know. I'm glad you're doing well, that means you will enjoy this cycling warm-up we are about to tackle." He said accompanied with a funny big brother teasing laugh, he sought to lighten up the moment.

"No way Larry (that's what she called him when she was being assertive or serious)! I will NOT be cycling today! Do you know the last time I was in a cycling class?! Even I don't remember and what's even worse is I almost threw up the last time I attended one. Who does cycling as a WARM UP anyway?! NO, thanks I will just wait for you over on the treadmills." She said as she tried to quickly walk away before he stopped her, but she wasn't quick enough and he was prepared for her resistance.

He grabbed her arm, "Come on little sister, do it for me. Please, we're not just here to work out, but to spend some time together too. I've missed you little pesky!" He said laughing.

"Why can't we do our warm up on the treadmill?" She asked.

"Because that's not a vigorous enough warm up. Listen, we will only spend 30 minutes in the cycling class, scouts honor" He said with a warm smile while lifting his right hand with his three fingers raised, exhibiting the boy scout stance.

Outside of her mother, L.J. was the most stubborn person that she knew and when his mind was set, it was set, there was no convincing him otherwise so she gave in. "Ok, fine. Let's get this over with." She said following behind him dragging her feet.

He turned around, "Thank you sister!" He extended his right fist to her and she reluctantly bumped her fist against his—it was the classic celebratory fist bump. But, she didn't see a reason to celebrate. "I promise the rest of the workout I'll go easy on you."

"Yeah right!' She responded as she rolled her eyes. "Your definition of easy really isn't easy! Anyways, I don't need you to go easy on me, I just hate cycling class, but I'll be a good sport." She concluded.

After cycling class they put in a good long workout that included lifting weights and a warm down on the treadmill. It was L.J.'s arm day and they performed exercises to strengthen his arms. They talked non-stop like two teen girls during their entire weight lifting session.

They had so much catching up to do. Natalie was impressed with her increased endurance and so was L.J. Although she had some slip ups in the eating department she had been very consistent with her workouts for months. She started her workout either early mornings with Jason and when they weren't together right when she got home from work as to not fall off of her routine. She worked out for an hour, spending 30-45 minutes on cardio and then the remaining time strength training for the full hour. Natalie loved that she was actually seeing results in her endurance, she wasn't losing weight as fast as she had hoped, but it was coming off slowly and she was losing inches. If she could just get her eating under control then she knew she would see the results she wanted to see before her big day.

Natalie filled her brother in on her engagement and her new life as Jason's finance. "You know I never thought I'd find someone to love me, the way he does L.J. It's so deep and strong. Sometimes it frightens me because I wonder if he will ever......" She paused, feeling her fears boiling over. "I just wonder if I'm enough." She said solemnly.

L.J, set his weight aside and interjected, "Listen! Of course he will! You're a great girl, I mean woman and any man would be blessed to have you! Besides, he knows he better not hurt you!" He said flexing his muscles. Natalie laughed. L.J. was the one person she could be brutally honest with and he trusted the same in her.

L.J. continued to listen intently to her as he lifted weights, many of her concerns he had heard many times over the years, but he didn't mind, he loved his sister.

After Natalie finished taking L.J. down the memory lane of her life for the past twelve months, they switched roles and L.J. talked while Natalie listened. She loved hearing about how much he loved Lisa and Livia. He was always a family man. Natalie was proud of L.J., he was a great boyfriend to Lisa, a wonderful father to Livia and he was happy!

"Can you believe she has red hair? I was looking at some of my baby pictures and Livia looks identical to me when I was her age. Isn't that something?" She said enthusiastically.

"Yes it is remarkable and there isn't a prettier person for Livia to look like than my beautiful baby sister." He said with a smile. He was great at making her feel good about herself and feeding her ego.

"You should win the best big brother award, I mean really, you know how to make a girl feel special!"

They finished their workout and recovered lost time all in one. The workout took longer than normal because of their catch up conversation. She even got the opportunity to ask him what she had been longing to ask him since she had gotten engaged. She wanted him to be her maid of honor! It wasn't traditional, but Natalie wasn't the most traditional girl. L.J. was a little weird-ed out by the idea at first, but there wasn't anything he wouldn't do for her. After being at the gym for almost three hours they had mended the broken areas in their relationship and was ready to rebuild again. He had explained to her why he disappeared from her and she shared with him her hurt over his disappearance to which he gave her a heart-felt apology that provoked her to tears. Neither of them spoke of Cheryl and it was just as well, their time together was well spent.

Chapter

19

<u>**A WOMAN'S INSECURITIES**</u>

Driving home Natalie was bouncing on the inside, the time with her brother was a success and now she was ready to see her man! She hoped he was at her condo. She couldn't wait tell him about her day.

Natalie walked through the door to her handsome fiancé sitting on the couch with remote in hand and flipping through the television. He gave her the biggest smile and she lit up. No one could make her feel more loved and at peace with just one smile. "Hi honey! What a pleasant surprise! How long have you been waiting for me? I hope not long," Natalie said with a huge smile as she came over to him to plant a greeting kiss on his lips.

"Hello my dear! I haven't been waiting very long. A little over 30 minutes maybe, I knew you and L.J. had a lot catching up to do and since both of you are conversationalist I figured you'd be gone awhile. Don't you just love how well I know you?! He said with a little chuckle and Natalie joined in.

"Awe honey you're so sweet and considerate! Baabyyy, I want to hug you, but let me go shower first, I smell like a sweaty rhino on a hot summer day at the zoo," she said as she turned to walk towards her bedroom.

Jason grabbed her before she could escape and wrapped his arms gently around the waist. "Honey you know your smelliness has never bothered me, I love a woman who smells like a sweaty rhino, it turns me on," he said waving his hand in front of his nose and giggling as he gave her a big kiss. Natalie surrendered a nervous laugh. He was funny, but she couldn't enjoy it as much because she wanted to avoid his advances. She tried to squeeze out of his grip because she knew what that meant, he wanted sex and she wasn't ready.

"Honey, please let me go shower," Natalie replied.

"At least let me join you. I haven't showered yet and I smell like a tooth that's caked with five day old food and needs a root canal," Jason said trying to get Natalie to loosen up and laugh a bit. Because he was a dentist his jokes typically consisted of corny dentist humor.

Natalie smiled, finally breaking free of his grip, "No honey, relax I'll be out shortly then you can shower after me."

"My love, do you know what today is? It's Tuesday. Yesterday was Monday and Monday is the day that we normally have some fun in the bedroom," he nonchalantly said trying not to sound pathetic and needy. Natalie enjoyed pleasing her fiancé, but she hated him gawking at the body she loathed and for that very reason she hadn't been able to enjoy sex—although she pretended like she did. She was in love with him, no doubt, but that part she could do without. The events from the night before left them both boggled, she forgot about their scheduled Monday night 'session' and right now, she just wasn't in the mood.

"Oh yes, yes, you're right!" She responded trying to sound happy. "Okay, yeah," she continued. "Let me shower *alone* and when I get out I will take good care of you," she said flirtatiously and then threw a sexy smile at him that just looked awkward. She needed to buy herself a little time to channel her sexy, confident and bold Queen Latifah alter ego which would make her feel more at ease. Three years into their relationship she had finally gotten him to a place where he was okay with having sex once a week which was a big leap for him because they were having sex three times a week.

Natalie had chosen Monday because she wanted her weekend to be free of any work and for her—sex was work. Jason never knew the real reason why she had chosen Monday, she guarded it, because she knew if she told him it would damage his ego.

"Please honey, let me join you! I promise it will be fun!" Jason said.

Fun for who? Natalie thought. Moving quickly past him, she gathered her night clothes and responded with, "I can't wait to tell you about the meeting with my brother. We had a great time!" Natalie said changing the subject. She walked past him again and went into the restroom, closing the door behind her. She leaned her back up against the restroom door, for the moment she felt safe from any sexual advances that lay behind the door. She hated being intimate in the shower, with all that bright light shining down on her. Give her a nice, pitch black room and she was in sexual ecstasy.

Whew, thank goodness I escaped! Or so she thought.

Jason sat confused, he wasn't sure what had just happened, but he had a plan! Natalie slowly undressed, her body was still aching from the workout with L.J. She stood in front of the mirror naked, silently reciting the confession that was on her mirror while she let the water run until it was hot and steamy in the restroom.

She kept trying to make her mind focus on the confession and getting into a confident place, but all she could think about was the pressure Jason just put on her for sex when really all she wanted was to have a long stimulating conversation while eating some pizza, fries, and her favorite dessert, strawberry ice cream!

Still reciting what she could remember from her confession, she stepped into the shower and hoped that by the time she got out she would be ready.

Then she heard a noise, it was the bathroom door closing. "Jason? Are you there?" Natalie asked. Before she could get his name out again, she felt a presence in the shower with her and kissing her breasts. Her eyes where shut tight, she had just put shampoo in her hair and was massaging it out.

"Jason what are you doing!?" Natalie asked. But Jason wouldn't utter a word, he just continued to slowly drape her body in soft wet kisses. He proceeded up her neck and Natalie began to moan. She still kept her hands in her hair with her eyes closed tightly, partially because she didn't want to get soap in her eyes and partially because she was afraid to see him, seeing her *naked*. He eased his way up and removed her hands from her head as the warm water cascaded down her spine.

"Jason what on earth are you doing!?" Natalie asked once again, more firmly this time in hopes that her tone would evoke an answer, but Jason stayed tight lipped. He was thankful that he came in at just the right time, with shampoo in her hair she was helpless and he loved every minute of it.

Natalie wasn't as controlling as Cheryl in the sense that she needed to control others, but she did want to control everything that happened to her and it was difficult for her to allow things to 'just happen'.

After he placed her hands to her side, he leaned her head back gently into the stream of the shower and allowed the water to flush the soap out of her hair. He massaged his fingers through her long and flowing red hair as he looked at her adoringly with her eyes still bolted tight, he washed every speck of shampoo out of her hair.

"Please Jason let me do that, you won't get all the shampoo out." Natalie insisted. Still silent, he kissed her lips and then wiped her eyes with a small towel that was hanging over the shower door. She looked up at him innocently, he had done many sweet things throughout the life of their relationship, but that was one of the sweetest! He was a romantic at heart and knew how to treat a lady.

That was exactly what she needed to loosen her up, she was ready to love him now. *Why do I get so fearful? He truly loves me, all of me.*

She thought as she let go and allowed herself to be loved. She was reminded that sex with him wasn't a chore but a privilege. She rose up on her tippy toes and kissed his lips and their tongues met. Jason reached behind her and turned the water off. Natalie grabbed a towel to cover up, but he gently pulled it away and dropped it on the shower floor. Natalie looked perplexed, she wasn't sure what was about to happen, but she was ready to follow his lead. He guided her out of the shower and into the bedroom their bodies still dripping wet. He tenderly laid her across the bed gently and she forgot all about how much she weighed or even that they both were laying their wet bodies across her perfectly made bed. She lovingly gave her freedom over to him and let him take charge as he made love to her in a way that she hadn't ever known.

Chapter

20

<u>"I LOVE YOU NATALIE ROSE ROBERTS!"</u>

They lay in each other's arms, passion still burning hot between the two of them, she raised up and asked, "Jason, where did that come from? Tonight, what was that all about? I've never experienced you like that before."

Jason looked her deep in her eyes, thinking of the best way to respond. "Get up, come with me!" He said grabbing her hand and leading her quickly into the closet.

"Wait Jason, let me grab my robe!" She said frantically reaching for it.

"You won't need it! Hurry! Come on babe!" Jason said motioning for her to enter the closet with him.

"Honneeyyy! What are you doing?" She asked.

"Babe, just come quickly!" He responded standing in the closet doorway. Natalie walked over slowly to the closet. *I wish he'd stop staring at me. This is so embarrassing. I'll walk slower so nothing jiggles.* She said within herself. She looked away as she walked towards the closet, she didn't want to make eye contact. *Maybe if I don't look at him, he won't see me. What are you thinking? You're not five anymore Natalie! Just because you don't look at him doesn't mean you somehow disappear and he no longer sees you. Just hurry and get to the closet.* She wrestled in her head.

"Come on honey," he said grabbing her hand and pulling her in the closet.

"Jason! What are we...?" Jason put his finger over her lips before she could finish.

"I want you to stand in front of this mirror and look at yourself," he said as he pulled her in front of him and they stood in front of the full length mirror in Natalie's closet.

"No, Jason! What are you doing? I know what I look like, I don't need to stand in front of this mirror. This is strange. I'm getting back in bed. Come join me, please," Natalie pleaded with Jason hoping she could persuade him to stop whatever he was doing, but it didn't work. She wasn't sure what he was up to, but she didn't like it!

Jason turned her around to face him, looking her intensely in her eyes and holding her shoulders he said, "Honey just give me a few minutes of your time, I promise it won't take long. I want you to see something with me."

"What could I possibly see, Jason? I know what my naked body looks like. Please, stop this! Whatever it...." He put his finger lightly over her mouth once again and slowly turned her around to face the mirror.

"Trust me," He whispered softly in her ear. With that one small gesture she felt secure and she allowed him to guide her, unsure, but she knew she was safe with him. Anticipating his next request, she observed her reflection in the mirror looking just as he had asked her to.

"I love you Natalie Rose Roberts soon to be Mrs. Jason Jacobs! Do you understand what that means? I'll tell you. Out of all the women, I CHOOSE you! From the first day I saw you walk into your brother's dorm room I knew you were the one. Your strawberry curly red hair bounced as you walked." He held her hair in his hands as he spoke examining each strand while his words carried them both down memory lane. "A thin head band adorned your luscious beautiful hair. I remember what you wore that day too, a black skirt with a black tank on the inside and a yellow cardigan with white pock-a-dots, pearl earrings and a pearl bracelet with little black heels."

She looked at him, tears filled her eyes, *how had he remembered that and with such detail,* she wondered. He continued, "And when you looked at me with those piercing green eyes, I had to know you, to be a part of your world. Something in you was calling to me and I wanted to love you the first time I laid eyes on you! Even though your brother threatened me over and over I couldn't resist you, it was like you were a magnet and I was drawn to you." They both chuckled!

"You were a hard shell to crack, shy and reserved. While other woman practically threw themselves at me with interest you weren't phased or intimidated by me one bit. But why would you be impressed? You, this beautiful rarity, more special than any woman I had ever laid eyes on. You had this amazing confidence about you!" She couldn't believe that what he saw as confidence was really insecurities wrapped in a shroud of fear, but she liked how he saw it.

He continued, "I love you!" He said as he touched her heart. "I love you Natalie Rose Roberts!" Jason exclaimed as he held his hand pressed to her heart while pressing the back of her naked body firmly against his. He continued, "Whatever you see in this mirror that you don't like doesn't matter to me, I was made to love you *forever*! You don't have to try to understand my love for you, why it exists or why I choose you. It exists because you do. I love all of you and that will never change from today until the end of time. You bring me joy and you make me happy and I will spend the rest of my life loving you and protecting you and no other woman will ever have my heart because this," he held his hand over her heart, "is connected to this," as he turned her around and placed her hand over his heart.

Jason turned her back around to face the mirror again. "Look at your reflection Natalie, you are the most beautiful woman to me. You are beautiful Natalie and if you never lose another pound I will love you just the same. You asked what tonight was about, tonight was about this," he said with his hand still on her heart. Tonight was about you feeling the security my love has for you, no more fear, no more worry and knowing that making love with you has nothing to do with what you see, but it has everything to do with what I see. And what I see is my love, my heartbeat."

Natalie allowed the hot tears to flow from her eyes as she looked in the mirror at her reflection and for the first time she no longer loathed the image looking back at her, she knew that she wasn't just a beautiful face, but a beautiful person.

Natalie followed Jason back to the bed overwhelming fulfilled. She rested her head in the crease of his forearm. They lay silently, she spun his words in her head like a turn table, remixing and replaying the words over and over again. Jason still recovering from the workout he just put in, she knew he would be fast asleep soon. Within minutes she looked up at him now asleep and breathing heavily, border line snoring. She gazed at him while he slept, smoothing his dark hair away from his forehead. She watched carefully as each hair smoothly glided through her fingers.

She lay back down on her pillow still resting in the assurance of his words. His words were like freedom, they freed her to the possibility that she could be okay just the way she was. It wasn't the validation of his words that affected her so deeply, but rather the acceptance. Happiness erupted on the inside of her and for the first time it wasn't accompanied with an impulse to eat. She finally realized that beauty wasn't found in a smaller size dress size—she didn't have to be a size 10 to be beautiful, she was beautiful right now, right in the skin she is in!

Natalie's earliest memories of her mother was of her being displeased with her. There was always something that she wanted Natalie to change. When she was a little girl it was her curly red hair and freckles. "Somehow you must've inherited this curly red hair and awful freckles from your father's side of the family!" She would even turn her cruelty into humor, "Don't you just wish you could scrub those freckles off your face?" She would ask Natalie followed by a little chuckle. Natalie never knew how to respond so she would say nothing as she absorbed blow after blow of her mother's brutality. Then finally she discovered a way to cope—good food!

Natalie didn't realize her coping mechanism would turn into a life long struggle, that it would cause people to judge her, hate her, talk about her, pity her, blind themselves to who she really was, and cause a love hate relationship with one thing that helped her get through so many difficult patches in her life.

Jason's words released her to a new perspective, she wasn't quite sure where it would lead, but she was ready for the ride! She loved him for reasons she couldn't explain and reasons she could. He was her perfect fit! She felt her most liberated with him. And that night he emancipated her from the cage of pressure from her mom and the world, she had never known such deliverance! One thing she knew for sure is that she was going to have to reevaluate some things, one huge thing was *how she saw herself!*

She drifted off to sleep cocooned in some of the most beautiful words that her ears had ever heard—words that gave her life, a new life so to speak!

Chapter

21

BIG TRASH DAY

Although she hadn't gotten much sleep, Natalie woke up the next morning refreshed she felt like she had taken a concoction of Red Bull, 5 Hour Energy, Rockstar, AMP, and Full Throttle energy drinks! Jason had already left for work. Natalie glanced over at the pillow where he had slept and found a hand written letter that simply read:

Thanks for last night, you were quite the acrobat! I left a $5.00 tip on the night stand for services I would like to have rendered tonight! Thank you!

Sincerely,

One Satisfied Customer

She read the letter then burst into laughter, *no one would ever guess him to be such a jokester,* she thought. She put the letter down and headed to the kitchen for breakfast. Natalie stood in the kitchen in front of the refrigerator with door wide open in a daze! She was frozen! She didn't know what to do. A frantic rage swept over her and she cleared everything out of her refrigerator, all the bacon, frozen chicken, eggs, the left over spaghetti from a few nights ago, left over pizza, she emptied a carton of milk in the sink, and she continued until it was bare. Then she rushed over to her pantry and cleared it of all the boxes of cereal, oatmeal, bread, potato chips, breakfast bars, wine, and she continued until it was bare. Her trash can was full and overflowing with a swamp of food surrounding it.

Natalie sat down on the ground next to the trash can. She was out of breathe and oblivious to what had happened. An impulse had rushed over her and she just went with it. She thrust her head into her hands and begin to sob deep and loud! She didn't understand what was happening, one minute she was happy, laughing even and now she was on the floor dry heaving with exhaustion from crying so hard. After about ten minutes of non-stop crying, as quickly as the bizarre episode had started—it stopped! She sat there awhile longer attempting to process what she had just done and why. Natalie was empty and drained from all the crying. She wiped her tears and the drainage of snot that had leaked from her nose with the sleeve of her pajamas.

Finally able to pull herself together she stood up and looked around at the damage she had done. The refrigerator door was still wide open and the sensor was beeping loudly from being left open. The pantry door stood wide open as well, it looked like a pack of wild, angry, and starving raccoons had ransacked her kitchen!

"What have I done?" She asked herself in a low mutter.

Before she could began the process of cleaning up her mess, she was stunned by a loud ringing nearby. It was her home phone. She went to retrieve it from the counter and saw the name and number scroll across. She let out a loud sigh, contemplating whether to answer it or not, her finger hit "answer"! Normally she felt anxiety when her mother called, but this time there was nothing, she was numb. What had just taken place on her kitchen floor had sucked the life out of her. She had no emotions to give!

Natalie hadn't realized she was sitting with the phone to her ear not saying a word until she heard the voice on the other end say, "Um, helloooo? Hello Natalie, are you there? Helloooo?"

Natalie finally responded, "Oh hi mom." Her voice still monotone!

"I'm doing well Nat! That's kind of you to ask!" Cheryl responded sarcastically.

Natalie cleared her throat, she didn't need any trouble for her mother—she was exhausted.

"I'm glad you are doing well! Sorry I didn't ask, I'm not feeling well today. I think I'm catching a cold." She lied, but she hoped that would end the conversation.

Cheryl could hear the weakness in her voice, but it wasn't enough to alarm her. She was on a nosey mission and she was going to sculpt away at Natalie until she got all the information she wanted.

Cheryl overlooked what Natalie had said and responded with, "I thought you said you would call me back?"

"No mom, I don't remember saying that. I'm really feeling horrible, I'm going to go lay down for a few minutes before I have to go to work. Is there something you called to tell me, specifically?

"Oh honey, I'm sure those little germ buckets got you sick. Why don't you just take the day off and get some rest, mommy can come over, make you soup and take care of you. Wouldn't that be fun?" Cheryl responded.

NO! Not, really! Natalie answered in her head.

Cheryl continued, nonchalantly, "Maybe that's God's way of letting you know you're supposed to be doing something greater with your life."

Natalie couldn't bear to hear one more word, she cut her off before she could spit out another ignorant sentence. "What?! What in the world are you saying? Are you saying God MADE me sick because I'm a TEACHER of children?"

"Now, Nat. You're overreacting again! I simply stated what I stated, it really isn't that big of deal," Cheryl responded casually. She wasn't seeking to make her upset, she just wanted to shake her up a little and it more than worked!

Instantly avoiding Natalie's response and transferring the situation back over to Natalie, Cheryl said, "Well, I won't keep you long since it sounds like you don't want to talk to me anyway." Natalie rolled her eyes on the other end of the phone, *is she really trying to lay a guilt trip on me?*

Cheryl cleared her throat, easing into her next sentence, "I heard you met with your brother yesterday. Sooo how did it go?"

Natalie's eyes got big, *how could she have known that*, she wondered. *On second thought I don't even want to know so I better not ask.* "Yes, mother we did meet and it went well. Mom, I really don't feel like talking right now. Remember, I don't feel well?"

"Oh yeah that's right. Ok, well maybe we can catch up and talk about it over dinner, after you, your dad, and your *best friend* meet up to look for your dress." She said best friend mockingly, she liked Courtney, but she was always jealous of their relationship. Cheryl had always longed for a best friend type relationship with her daughter, but she never knew how to develop it. She continued, "I'm still not sure why I'm not invited. Everyone knows that a girl's mother must be a part of the wedding dress selection."

"Mother, I'd love to have you come, but you take over and I can't see clearly what I want for hearing what you want for me. If you could come and not voice your opinion so much you're more than welcome to join us. If that's difficult for you then sure we can meet up for dinner with everyone and I'd love to have Jason join us as well," she said in the same tone she uses to talk to her students when she's trying to reason with them when they're being difficult.

"Fine Natalie, I'll meet you for dinner," Cheryl conceded feeling frustrated and defeated. No matter how hard she tried, there was no way she could avoid voicing her opinion—it was simply who she was.

Somehow, she had to find a way to relate to her better or risk losing her relationship with her as she had done with L.J.

"Thank you mom, that's so nice of you!" Natalie exclaimed. She was fully aware of how hard that was for her and equally big of her to be willing to allow her to have a special moment free from her opinion— rather her scrutiny. In all of her dysfunction, Natalie had to admit that Cheryl was trying in her own way. They were both learning a new language and a new way to be with one another, for Cheryl it was scary giving up so much of her forced influence, but for Natalie it was invigorating.

"We should be done around 7pm. I need to try on a few more dresses, Courtney needs to be fitted for her dress and we'll be done after that. You want to meet, say, around 7:30?" Natalie asked.

"I suppose that will work," she responded still a little solemn that she wasn't going to get to share in one of her daughter's special moments. Cheryl continued, "What do you think about trying that new Italian restaurant? The one downtown on Grand Blvd."

"Oh that would be GRAND mom! No pun intended," she laughed trying to cheer her mom up. With uncomfortable silence on the other end of the phone she continued, "I've heard some great things about it. You're speaking of Ristorante Bonaroti, right?"

"Yes, that's the place," Cheryl responded dryly. "Listen, I'm going to let you get off the phone so you can rest. Feel better and I'll see you tonight." Cheryl concluded and waited for Natalie to respond with her good-byes.

Natalie was puzzled at her mom's response, she wasn't sure if she was being manipulative or if she was really hurt by not being able to come to her dress fitting. Even more shocking, Cheryl actually showed a little sympathy towards her, which was a rarity. Cheryl had gone from being her usual self to being humble. In all her days Natalie had never heard her mother forfeit a conversation without getting what she wanted and she wouldn't have ever bowed out of an important event for her.

Although Cheryl was very opinionated, strong willed, controlling, and judgmental, she was very supportive in her own way and she would've never missed an opportunity to support her children or husband. She prided herself on being her family's support system, she sometimes referred to herself as 'the glue'. Natalie, baffled as to what her reply should be, simply said slowly, "Okay. See you soon!"

They both hung up. Cheryl sat on her couch as daunting chills ran all through her and the feeling of loneliness swaddled her. She was frighteningly more aware than ever that she had to make some changes or risk losing all the people she loved most.

She and Larry had had problems in their marriage off and on for years, but this was the first time he was fed up with what he called her 'irrational behavior'. It had gotten so bad, most days she was surprised that he even came home. Larry had been sleeping in the guest room for months, after a huge fallout between the two of them. This wasn't the first time he decided to sleep in the guest room, but this was the first time that he hadn't returned in months, not even for sex.

Cheryl had secretly been seeing a counselor that a friend had recommended and even included daily prayer in her behavior management regiment. At this point she willing to try anything, she wanted desperately to change. She hadn't told anyone about her life styles updates, she didn't want to get anyone's hopes up in case it didn't work. That was her fear—that she couldn't change! She had been the same way for 54 years and even though for the sake of her family she wanted to be better, she wasn't sure she actually could be.

Cheryl picked up the phone and cleared her throat she heard the other person on the phone say hello. "Hello," she said in a monotone mutter. She continued, "Can you see me today? I know its short notice, but I desperately need your help."

"I'll squeeze you in during my lunch. How does noon sound?" The voice on the other ended responded.

"Thank you! I'll see you soon!" Cheryl responded gratefully.

Chapter

22

<u>BEAUTY IS….</u>

It was fitting time at Elegance Bridal and Couture and Natalie was nervous! She was glad that her dad and Courtney had come along to help her make the selection. To Natalie's surprise she had dropped another dress size, she was hoping she would have been a little smaller by the time of her last fitting, but she was proud of herself for making it as far as she had considering all the stress she had been under lately. She had narrowed her selection down to three dresses and she was sending Vicki the owner of Elegance into a tail spin of frustration with her unreasonable bridezilla demands. Vicki was not only a friend of the family, but she had been best friends with Cheryl for the last 30 years and was Godmother to L.J. and Natalie. Now on her seventh visit, Vicki was becoming weary, she hoped today was the day she made her selection.

"Oh God mommy this is it! This is the dress!" Natalie said with great excitement as she smoothed the dress down on either side and glared at herself in the mirror, looking at her image from all angles, the front, both the sides and the back.

Vicki had agreed to personally design her dress to her liking, but she was afraid that the requests Natalie was making was a tall order not for her ability to produce, but for Natalie's ability to fit it. Vicki wanted to make sure that Natalie was sure of what she was asking.

"Natalie, are you sure you still want the measurements we discussed several months ago?" Vicki asked.

"I'm certain! I promise your work will not be in vain," Natalie assured her putting her hand on Vicki's arm.

"It's not my work I'm concerned about. What if you don't have a dress on your wedding day?! Are you going to save me when your mother kills me BECAUSE you don't have a dress ON YOUR WEDDING DAY!?" She said animatedly in an attempt to amuse herself to ease some of her irritation, but it didn't help much.

Natalie laughed hoping to relieve Vicki of her nerves, "I assure you all will be well, I will have a wedding dress and no one will have to die on my wedding day. Now, come, let's show everyone this gorgeous dress!" Natalie linked her arm to Vicki's arm as they walked out of the dress room arm and arm.

"Okay everyone feast your eyes on THE dress!" Natalie announced as she stepped around the corner.

"Oh my goodness, Lisa?! Awe and you brought Livia?! What an amazing surprise!" Natalie said excitedly. She embraced Lisa and reached her hands out to hold Livia. At first Livia pulled away, but Natalie had a beautiful way with children, it only took Natalie two tries and Livia was in her arms.

"How did you know about today?" Natalie asked Lisa. "I wanted you to come, but I figured you might be too busy," Natalie said. She offered the words "too busy" as a legitimate excuse for her. Natalie knew Lisa was mostly home with the baby, truth was she was afraid Lisa wouldn't come. She wasn't quite sure how Lisa felt about their meeting a few nights before and Natalie was concerned that Lisa might be upset about how things turned out.

"I'm sure you will be surprised to know that it was your mother who told me about today," Lisa replied. Natalie gasped and looked over at her dad in disbelief!

"It's true, neither of us told her," Larry said as he looked over to Courtney who nodded her head in agreement.

"We were just as shocked as you when Lisa told us," Courtney chimed in.

"Dad is something wrong with mom? Is she sick or something?" Natalie asked with panic on her face.

"No sweetie your mother is fine," he chuckled.

"She's exhibiting some odd behavior, but in a good way though. I spoke with her this morning and was pleasantly surprised with our conversation," Natalie explained.

"I was shocked to hear from her this morning myself. She even apologized to me for how she behaved the other night AND for how she's treated me the last few years," Lisa said.

"No way, MY mother apologize—and to you?!" Natalie said shock vibrating from voice. Larry gave her a bizarre look, despite all they had been through he always remained devoted to his wife.

Natalie, catching the peculiar look Larry gave her, addressed him. "I'm sorry dad, I don't mean to sound facetious, I'm just really flummoxed about mom's behavior and in all fairness I have good reason to be. Wouldn't you agree? Natalie rationalized.

Larry caught a glimpse of his expression in the mirror behind Natalie. He hadn't wanted to alarm anyone and certainly not Natalie during such a critical moment in her life. "I understand dear, let's talk about all this another time. For now, let's look at this amazing dress you're wearing darling! You look beautiful!" he said admiring his daughter and steering everyone's curiosity away from his wife all at once.

Natalie stopped her mind from racing and thinking about her mother. She kissed Livia on the cheek and handed her back to Lisa and said, "I'm so glad you and Livia are here!" Natalie smiled, their presence flooded her with hopes that they could all really be a functional family. She basked in the beautiful moment.

Natalie walked over to her dad, looked up at him and said, "Do you really think so daddy?" She asked in the sweetest little girlish voice possible. The pure love that he freely gave her, brought her back to a very childlike state.

"Oh absolutely kiddo! You are going to be the most beautiful bride ever!" He responded, as Vicki, Courtney and Lisa chimed in their agreement.

Natalie stood up high on tippy toes and kissed her dad on the cheek, "Thank you daddy!"

"You all certainly know to make me feel like the luckiest girl ever," Natalie said locating her reflection in the mirror. She blushed. There was a totally different girl looking back at her, the image was still the same—*yet different*! She saw it—what they had seen! She *finally* saw herself! The woman Jason had introduced to her to the night before. The one her father had adorningly called beautiful her whole life! It was her and she *was* beautiful, not just a beautiful face, but a whole entire beautiful woman.

For so many years her confidence was literally a vibration of who her dad had taught her she was, but it wasn't who she really believed she was. But, that day in the bridal shop, looking at her reflection in a wedding dress amongst people who truly loved her, in front of the one man who had spoken *beautiful* life into her since she could remember—she believed! In fact it wasn't just a belief, she knew it!

"You're right dad, I am beautiful! I AM BEAUTIFUL!" She declared, her eyes still fixated on a woman she was really meeting for the first time. She let the words roll off her tongue and plant themselves deep in heart. Tears glided down her cheek as she began to embrace and sit inside the words she had just spoken.

Courtney felt her face heating up as hot tears ran from her eyes, she had never heard Natalie speak about herself and with such conviction. Courtney went to Natalie and gently eased the hair on either side of her face behind her ears. Their eyes met. Courtney wiped away Natalie's tears with a kleenex and gave her a long consoling hug. Something wonderful was happening on the inside of her friend and it brought her great pleasure to witness it. No one knew more than Courtney the agony Natalie had suffered through for so many years.

It's tragic when everyone including the world makes your private issues your public shame! Courtney recalled a time when she and Natalie were in college and shared a dorm room. Natalie came into the dorm room crying hysterically and the words she spoke Courtney never forgot. Through heartache and weeping she said, "Courtney, you may never understand this feeling of having the whole world bully you all because you don't fit their standard of beauty." Courtney never knew what caused her friend so much grief that day she just listened to her pain and allowed her to cry on her lap as she comforted her as best she could. But, to see her go from that and many days like it, to the present day— embracing herself and her beauty moved Courtney to tears!

Vicki walked over and wrapped her arms around the pair as they hugged. Larry walked over kissed Natalie on the forehead and wrapped his arms around the three. Natalie peaked through the loving arms that held her tight to see Lisa who had diverted all her attention to Livia in an effort to avoid felling awkward and left out.

Natalie motioned for Lisa to come over, "Please," she said softly. Lisa walked over and Larry pulled her and his grandbaby into the circle of love. Natalie let out a sigh of relief, "Now this is a dressing fitting!"

She said laughing through her tears while everyone joined in with heartfelt laughter.

Chapter

23

<u>FORGIVENESS</u>

The months swirled around quickly to the day that Jason and Natalie had waited for—their wedding day! Natalie was marrying the love her life and she couldn't be more ecstatic or more anxious! She sat gazing at her image in the mirror as her stylist finished the last details of her wedding hairstyle. She was so pleased to be looking at a woman she admired, loved and even celebrated! Months ago, she couldn't have even found those sentiments for herself, but she come through a lot and the woman sitting in her chair was totally different than who she had known just months prior!

Amidst her concoction of emotions, the one that spoke the loudest was nervousness. Her palms sweated profusely as she rubbed them against the fabric of her robe endeavoring to wipe some of the moisture away. She couldn't believe what was about to happen, as she watched all her bridesmaids shuffle around the room preparing for *her* wedding. *Her* wedding, a day she had always hoped for as a young girl, but didn't believe a man would actually want to marry her. Natalie's eyes kept welling up with tears and to prevent them from rolling down her face she would slowly roll her eyes to the tops of her lids to push them back. She didn't want to be an emotional mess on her wedding day even though she was very close to becoming just that.

Although it had been a very tumultuous several months leading up to her wedding, she was at peace with where she had come in life. It had taken her twenty-five years to get to the space she was in and she wasn't going to allow anyone to take her treasured moment away from her, not even her mother whom she hadn't spoken to after the huge argument they had at the restaurant the day of her final wedding dress fitting. Natalie had wished she could take it all back, but the peace of mind she had experienced since her mother wasn't a consistent agitation in her life had been paradise. She hadn't realized how much control her mother had in her life just by simply being in it. No matter how much she tried to displace it, counsel it away, self-help it out, her desire to please her mother consumed her when they were in close proximity of one another. Now that she was free of Cheryl's influence she finally got to find out who she really was and to her surprise she really liked what she found!

They had the worst squabble ever. It was so bad that Larry, L.J. and even Jason begged them to take some time apart until after the wedding. They were all fully aware of how Cheryl affected Natalie and as a soon to be bride she didn't need any extra stress from a continually straining relationship with her mother.

The time away had equally been good for Cheryl although she dreaded everyday of not having access to Natalie, it made her appreciate Natalie—just the way she was. The break from Natalie and L.J.'s abrupt sabbatical gave her time to really evaluate how she needed to progress with her family. She had debated for weeks if she was even going to go to Natalie's wedding. She didn't want her presence to destroy Natalie's experience.

Natalie's wedding was being held at a lovely mansion, it was a friend of the family who owned a beautiful 13,000 square feet home that sat on a private lake that everyone lovingly called The River House of New Haven. The beautiful immaculate home had every amenity imaginable, it had its own library, game room, movie theater, three massive kitchens, six restrooms, a pool with at club house, sauna, steam room, six car garage, and six bedrooms. Outside by the river was a beautiful garden with 12 different types of exquisite flowers delightfully dancing in the slight breeze that lifted off of lake. In the garden overlooking the lake was where Jason and Natalie would become one.

Natalie slipped on her wedding gown and allowed her body to wrap up in the soft fabric as it gently laid against her skin. It felt good and fit perfectly. She looked breathtakingly beautiful! Viewing her image caused waterworks to surface to her eyes once again. The first time she had tried on a wedding dress she loathed the image she saw, now she loved it! She was radiant in her white wedding gown! Her hair was swept away in an exquisite chignon with a few wispy red ringlets of hair draping the sides of her face. Her makeup was flawless, which had to be touched up after several tears slipped passed her resistance and tumbled down her cheek.

Her bridesmaids stood around her in awe of her beauty. Courtney grabbed her hand to lead the group in a short prayer before the wedding planner came back to retrieve the ladies to march down the aisle. Before they could bow their heads in prayer a quiet knock sounded at the door.

Courtney shouted out politely, "Hold on one second please, we're almost ready!"

Recognizing the voice of the person on the other side of the door, she responded sheepishly, "Um Courtney, it's me. Can I come in please?"

Natalie immediately jerked her head up—she knew that voice. She stepped back from the circle of prayer and calmly walked to the door. She opened it and it was Cheryl on the other side. Natalie stood in astonishment, staring at her mother.

"Hello Natalie." Cheryl said humbly. "Oh my God you look stunning!" She said captured by her radiance while reaching out to touch Natalie's cheek. Natalie flinched, but allowed her to caress her face.

"Thank you mom," Natalie responded surprised that her mother was standing before her AND that she had *complimented* her.

Cheryl looked behind Natalie's shoulder and addressed Courtney and the other ladies in the room. "Ladies can I ask you to excuse the room? I need to talk to Natalie for a few minutes."

Natalie turned around to give Courtney and the ladies a nod to confirm that it was okay for them to leave the room. Courtney didn't want to leave Natalie alone with Cheryl, she hoped the outcome would be good, but with Cheryl you never knew what would happen next.

Courtney politely smiled at Natalie and replied, "Okay, I'll just be in the adjacent room if you need me."

Natalie directed her attention back to her mother.

"Natalie may I come in and sit down?" Cheryl asked. Without any words, Natalie opened the door up wide allowing her mother to enter.

Cheryl looked down at her feet bashful, "I won't take up much of your time. I-I just wanted to apologize to you, Jason and even Lisa. But I wanted to say I'm sorry to you first. I have been the most horrible version of myself for so many years that it had become the norm and my normal affected those around me and even caused many people to hate me, possible even you." Cheryl looked away ashamed. Forcing her eyes to locate Natalie's again she continued, "I was angry at myself, at my life and I took it out on everyone, but you got the brunt of bitterness! You were everything I wasn't, beautiful, smart, kind, courageous, and loving. I had so many unfilled dreams when I became a mom and I suppose, no I don't suppose, I did take it out on you."

Cheryl grabbed Natalie's hands and placed them in hers. "Nat, I beg of you, please forgive me for treating you so cruel for so many years. I tried to make you strive for perfection because I wanted you to go further than I ever did." She looked down at her hands that still had a tight grip of Natalie's hands; she was mortified by the next words that were to proceed out of her mouth. "But on the other hand I was jealous of you, you're like everything good all wrapped up in one person! People look at me and they see this woman they think has it all together, but inside there are so many broken, tarnished pieces that I've carried since childhood. I desperately wanted to do more with my life, but I couldn't because of choices I had made, so I silently envied you and I put pressure on you. That pressure pushed you away from me," she said, her voice now cracking as she struggled to push out the reminder of what she needed to say. "Natalie I just want you to know that I love you and I am so very proud of you! I see you just the way you are and you are and have always been a lovely person and despite how I have made you feel or what I have said, you truly are a beautiful young woman."

Natalie grabbed her mother and hugged her tightly, those words were priceless and they were all she ever wanted to hear. Cheryl let out a loud gasp, relieved that Natalie had accepted her apology. In the time they hadn't been speaking, Cheryl had given her life to Christ and she wasn't the same person anymore. Over the years she had tried to unsuccessfully change herself, but Jesus had done in one instance what she had tried to do for decades. Larry had a different wife and L.J, and Natalie had a changed mother!

Natalie breathed in deep. She held back her tears, she couldn't afford to ruin her make-up again it was almost time for her to meet her future husband. "Mom, I..." before she could get her sentence out the wedding planner barged in.

"Natalie, we have to go now! The wedding party is getting into position and your dad is on his way up to get you."

Natalie turned to her mother and lightly kissed her on the check and mouth the words, "Thank you."

Chapter

24

"I ABSOLUTELY DO!"

Natalie held her lavender and white flowered bouquet tightly in her hands as she fidgeted at the top of the staircase waiting for her father to retrieve her. The words that her mother had spoken still sat on her heart, but she couldn't afford to linger there with them she had a wedding to attend—hers.

Everyone in the wedding party was in place and waiting for her to appear. Jason and Natalie had a total of seven bridesmaids and groomsmen, four flower girls and Jason's dog as their ring barrier (with help of course). Then there was L.J. who had accepted the privilege of being her maid of honor. Natalie couldn't wait much longer she was antsy! Apparently, Larry was just as nervous, right when the music started up for the bridal party, he made a dash for the restroom. He could no longer contain his bowels.

In an effort to make everything run smoothly with no alarm to Jason, Natalie, or the guests, the wedding planner made each bridesmaid and groomsmen walk very slowly down the aisle and she asked the pianist to play equally as slow. Everyone was in position and still no Natalie had appeared as Larry was still locked away in the restroom. The entire gathering watched the entrance closely.

Natalie could hear the music, she knew the wedding party was in position, but still her dad hadn't arrived—she begin to panic. She looked over at her wedding planner with tears starting to well up in her eyes. She knew something wasn't right. Then she felt a presence staring at her. Natalie looked down at the bottom of the stair case and standing quietly at the end gazing at his beautiful daughter was Larry! Immediately her heart warmed up, and the panic fled. Seeing her dad gave her assurance—the day was going to be perfect!

 He had been her safe place her whole life and just the sight of him caused a feeling of security to surge all over her. He slowly climbed to the top of the stairs his eyes fixed on her the entire time. The wedding planner dabbed the little specks of tears that had pooled within her eyelids with a kleenex and then delivered her hand over to Larry. He took her hand and secured it around his arm. He smiled and she smiled back, but her eyes were still longing. Larry placed her hand at her side and wrapped his strong arms around her and she pressed her head into his chest. He lifted her head slightly and whispered in her ear, closing everyone out of their private moment. She laughed at his words of admiration, assurance, and love! They shared a smile once again and he gathered her face in his hands kissing her forehead then gently sliding the veil over her face. *They were both ready!*

"Honey you look gorgeous and that's an understatement," he said placing her hand around his arm again.

"Oh daddy, thank you! Thank you so much!" She replied in the most angelic and loving voice. That was a 'thank you' that stretched beyond that moment, it was a 'thank you' for everything he had been and everything he would continue to be in her life!

She exhaled, "Okay, I'm ready!" They walked slowly down the long winding staircase, step by step and side by side. After a year of being engaged she was ready to become Mrs. Jason Jacobs!

Clinging to her father's arm they stood outside the entry way of the outdoor garden, she gazed at all the beauty surrounding her. Seeing her bridesmaids, some of her most favorite women in the world, dressed in their white and lavender gowns and the men dressed so handsomely, the beautiful flower girls, the lovely flowers, and the scenic lake that glistened as white swans pranced on it caused a feeling of love to dance on the inside of her. The atmosphere was filled with love! She was startled back from her fairytale thoughts as the musical cue for her to come down the aisle chimed in and everyone stood to attention. Her legs where shaking underneath her dress, as she attempted to take her first step. She looked up at her father anxiously and he reinforced his grip over her hand that was cleaving to his arm, signaling to her that he had her and that everything was going to be okay. Redirecting her attention away from her nervousness and back to the steps she needed to take to reach her groom, he mouthed the words, "You look beautiful baby girl." She beamed so brightly that he could see her beautiful pearly white teeth gleaming from underneath her veil. The music was playing melodically as the full orchestra played on, everyone anticipating her first step. However, her feet remained glued to the ground. She was trying to shake her anxieties. *This needs to be perfect! Everything needs to be perfect!* She thought leaning over fumbling with her dress. The wedding planner came behind her to flare her dress out and straighten it once again.

Jason could see her, *why isn't she moving towards me,* a fearful thought flooded his mind. *Has she changed her mind?* His thoughts wrestled while he strained to not allow his feelings of panic to rush to his face.

Larry gently glided his hand across her hand that was still holding his arm. She rose to greet his face once again, she looked into his eyes and peace enveloped her once again. "Princess Pudding Pop it's time," he said in a very low gentle tone. Natalie locked and secured her arm underneath her father's as she allowed him to guide her to her groom. She closed her eyes tight for the first 10 steps, trying to calm herself, she wasn't prepared to look at everyone just yet, but she could hear their `Ah's and Oh's' she wasn't sure if it was the dress that captured their eyes or if it was her new appearance, but she wasn't ready to find out yet.

She finally made her way to the front and she looked at Vicki, who was crying. Her only God-daughter whom she had the privilege of watching blossom into a young lady was getting married and the dress that she specially contoured for Natalie—fit perfectly! It was a size 16! Natalie had done it and reached her wedding dress size goal!

The last person her eyes met before she was given to her groom was her mother. Cheryl's was weeping, a very rare occasion and even more surprising was that she allowed them to see her cry.

Customarily, Cheryl had never let people see her cry or get emotional. Natalie wanted to go to her and hug, but she had to keep her focus on her man, she had made him wait long enough. Natalie blew an air kiss to her mother and Cheryl grabbed it, placed her hands at her heart and smiled. *This feels so good!* Cheryl thought grinning and wiping her tears with a tissue.

Larry lifted his daughter's veil with a warm smile and a love beaming from his eyes, Natalie closed her eyes, basking in his love as he kissed her on the forehead once again. He released her to her groom and took his seat beside Cheryl. The wedding was beyond exquisite. Jason and Natalie where surrounded by flowers on either side of them—it was perfectly picturesque! It looked like something on the cover of a wedding magazine. The weather was perfect for a summer evening and at 7:42 p.m., not too far behind schedule, Jason shouted the loudest, "I absolutely DO!"

He was so excited he hadn't even waited to hear, "You may now kiss your bride!" He placed his hand gently behind her head and pressed his lips softly against hers. The pastor kindly declared, "Looks like you two love birds couldn't wait, carry on!" He said with a chuckle as everyone else joined in with sweet laughter. It was as if God himself had kissed the moment as the sun began to set behind them and the water sparkled ever so clear.

They kissed not once, not twice, but three times and each time was longer and more intense than the kiss before. The pastor hurried to interject before they went in for the fourth kiss, "I now introduce to you Mr. and Mrs. Jason Jacobs!" He announced to the world! There was hardly a dry eye as everyone clapped and cheered.

Chapter

25

"WHAT QUALIFIES AS BEAUTY?"

Pictures had been taken and Jason and Natalie had joined the reception. The wait staff were starting to clear the plates away as Jason's best man was up talking, he was the last to share in the line of people who had spoken about their union. Natalie squirmed in her seat as each person went up to the platform to speak. She kept wanting to get up and grab the microphone. The words Cheryl had spoken had remained in the back of Natalie's mind since Cheryl had visited her in her dressing room and she couldn't sit still anymore, she leaned into Jason and said, "Honey, I need to say something."

He looked at her puzzled for a few seconds then motioned for the wedding planner to bring the microphone over to where they were seated. Everyone turned their eyes to them, Jason stood up, grabbed the microphone and spoke into it, "You all have said such lovely words about me and my beautiful bride! I can't wait to spend the rest of my life with such a pure and amazing woman! Speaking of, my bride, Mrs. Natalie Jacobs has something she would like to share."

Natalie cleared her throat, her heart housed the words she just hoped her head could connect them well enough to articulate them clearly. She didn't want to offend anyone not even her mother, she had genuinely forgiven her and she hoped every word that proceeded out of her mouth conveyed that. She glanced at Cheryl and smiled a warm smile from her heart. Natalie slowly lifted the microphone to her mouth and looked at Jason who was watching her attentively. She loved the support she saw beaming from his eyes. Natalie breathed in deeply and then allowed the words to gradually emerge from her lips. "All my life I thought I was supposed to be consistently fixing something about myself, like I was some broken priceless piece of...of nothing! The world makes you believe if you're overweight you're not supposed to be happy, so I fought to achieve what 'they' expected of me. Then I realized I wasn't fighting to be healthy. I was fighting for society's acceptance, for my friends' acceptance, for my mother's love. My desire to lose weight had so little to do with me; it was all about everyone else and comparisons. How I looked compared to my skinny friends. What size I wore compared to the actress on the TV screen. What I ate in comparison to models who were full after eating two pieces of lettuce. But what if I desire variety and more than just salad and cucumbers? My pursuit to lose weight to look the way a society who knew nothing about me and cared nothing about me was making me fatter—the pressure made me eat more," She said looking down at her frame.

"I allowed myself to be governed by people's perception of me. We are all searching to be loved, to be accepted, to be valued, but one of the hardest pills to swallow is when you can't give those needs to yourself. When you wait for someone else's approval over your own! When you dress nice in hopes for someone to tell you that you look pretty today. That was me. I was searching for something from people that I couldn't stand in the mirror and see myself because I believed the world's opinion of me!" With tears streaming down her face, she continued, "What qualifies as beauty anyway? Is it your perception of me? Is it my perception of me or somewhere in between? What if I'm not beautiful and yet still I AM? There has to be something more to being beautiful than just this body and this face. Today, I stand before you and I'm not a size two, but I love the size I'm in and while I've lost weight the most important thing I've lost is fear, low self-esteem, insecurities, and self-doubt." She said with relief filling the burden of all the negative weight she had been carrying lift as she vocally denounced their control over her.

"Everyone needs someone who can see past all this exterior stuff and see inside here," Natalie said pointing at her heart. "It was my loving husband, Jason, who saw my true beauty and he made me see it! He recovered me and helped to restore me to the woman you see today! I'm no longer worried about people not liking me or drowning in the fear that my husband may one day fall out of love with me. I love me and I even *like* myself! Any adoration I receive outside of myself is an added bonus!" she said with a slight giggle. She was enjoying her new confidence!

"Lastly, I want to say I forgive everyone, EVERYONE!" She said looking deep into Cheryl's eyes who had been crying profusely during her whole speech.

Natalie then smiled warmly at Jason, who himself, began to tear up, he stood up and clapped loudly, ushering everyone into a standing ovation. Jason pulled her in for a tight embrace—he was so proud of her! Natalie was proud of herself, the fact that she never brought up anything her mom had done that contributed to her weight issues showed so much growth and proved that she really had forgiven her.

Chapter

26

THE LAST DANCE –Well NOT REALLY!

It was time for the father-daughter dance. Natalie glided towards Larry in her stunning fabulous wedding gown with her shoulders peering over the top, beautiful stones sparkled from the dress with each stride. He watched as her long train trailed behind her and his heart melted. Natalie once again morphed into his precious Princess Pudding Pop coming for a spin with him after a long day's work.

He placed her hand gently into his hand and they glided across the dance floor as though no one was watching. If there was a model father daughter relationship theirs was it. Standing at 5 foot 4 inches and with no heels on, she stood evenly at his chest, which is where she rested her head, listening to his heart beat as he continued to slowly glide her around on the dance floor. She began to reminisce on times past. They had shared so many great memories and she was grateful that he had always made her feel just the way she felt in that moment, beautiful and loved! It was his love that allowed her to know that even though she didn't always like the frame she was in, she deserved a man that would love every part of her the way he had. She lit up at the thought.

Out of Larry's peripheral view he saw someone walking closer and closer—it was Cheryl. Concern swept over him as he wasn't sure what she was going to do. She tapped him lightly on the shoulder, "Can I join in?" She asked softly. He looked down at Natalie who nodded her approval. They opened up their twosome to include a threesome, they danced and laughed as the song changed. Then L.J. came walking across the floor, Cheryl looked at him sheepishly, he hadn't said a word to her all night and she was sure he was still angry at her. He came and stood in front of her as Larry and Natalie looked on. No one was sure what was about to happen, but Natalie hoped it was good. Cheryl reached up with her right hand and gently rubbed L.J.'s face, he closed his eyes and welcomed her love.

"I'm so sorry son. I have hurt you so deeply. I was so stubborn. I was an ugly woman living a beautiful lie. I hope you can forgive me. I truly do love you so very much!" Cheryl repented. She had prayed for the opportunity to apologize to him, but she knew L.J. was just as stubborn as her. He wouldn't be as receptive as Natalie, he had to receive her in his own timing. She just hoped he would accept her apology.

L.J. had been watching her all night and he could see a clear difference in her. He reached down, scooped her up in his arms and gave her a big hug. She let out an exuberant laugh. She was overjoyed! What started out as a twosome turned into a circle of four. Everyone looked on enjoying the circle of love. Natalie motioned for Jason and L.J. motioned for Lisa who was holding Livia to join them. The dance turned into one huge family circle, as other family members and friends joined the celebration of love and forgiveness—and yes it was beautiful.

Cheryl looked over at Larry and said, "See honey, **no one** is ever too old to change!"

"You're right honey! You're so right!" He leaned down and gave her a long kiss, pulling her into himself for a tender embrace.

Coming Soon...

...And She Laughed ~ **Volume II**

Prelude...

<u>FREEDOM</u>

She was sitting erect on the floor, knees pressed tightly against her chest with her back against the door and palms planted firmly to the ground to keep her balance. Utilizing her body as an additional weight to keep him out, she could still feel the force of each bang his fist created with every blow to the bathroom door. She knew the door lock and her body could only keep him out for so long. He is a big guy and she is a small woman.

 She sobbed, pleading with him, "Please, I promise I will do better next time, please I beg you don't hit me again!" Fueled with rage and a half a bottle of vodka, he screamed derogatory names, cursing her over his loud hits to the door. Her face was still pulsating from the punch he had delivered to it moments ago. She prayed that was all the damage he would leave and they could go to the *"I'm sorry"* phase, but she had never seen him so angry!

Author Connection

VISIT ANESHASHARP.COM

❧ To Learn More About Anesha Sharp or Her Ministry and Business

❧ For Speaking Engagements and Book Signings

❧ To Sign Up For Anesha's Blogs

❧ To Purchase Additional Books and Materials Written By Anesha

To Contact Anesha directly call her at: 813-693-2293.